JAKE HENRY

A GUN FOR SHELBY

Complete and Unabridged

LINFORD
Leicester

First published in Great Britain in 2017

First Linford Edition
published 2018

A catalogue record for this book is available
from the British Library.

ISBN 978–1–4448–3791–9

Published by
F. A. Thorpe (Publishing)
Anstey, Leicestershire

Set by Words & Graphics Ltd.
Anstey, Leicestershire
Printed and bound in Great Britain by
T. J. International Ltd., Padstow, Cornwall

This book is printed on acid-free paper

This one is for Sam and Jacob.

And for David Whitehead
who's helped me from the start.

Author's Note.

While history tells a different story about the great southern general Joseph Shelby, what follows in the coming pages is all a figment of the author's imagination and not meant to be construed as true events.

The other point I'll make has to do with the settlement of Phoenix. The original settlement was, in fact, started in late 1867 and early 1868. It was officially recognized as a town on May 4, 1868, and the post office established on June 15 of that year. Therefore, the timeline in this story may be somewhat earlier (by a few months) than in real life.

In writing this story, the author has taken fictional license and created (hopefully) an exciting alternate twist to a tale of the man who became a legend.

Jake Henry, 2017.

1

'You, sir, are a cheat,' a well-dressed man with a southern accent accused as he lurched to his feet. His icy stare remained fixed on the solidly built man who sat opposite.

His accused had black hair and wore a low-crowned black hat tipped back on his head. A buckskin jacket covered a Union blue shirt; his pants matched the shirt and were tucked into black cavalry boots.

Savage's face hardened, and he stopped raking the pot towards himself across the battered tabletop. His brown eyes grew hard. 'And you shouldn't shoot your mouth off so freely. It's likely to get you killed.'

The other players eased their chairs back, the scraping noise on the floorboards almost deafening in the otherwise silent room.

Ned Tate's stare never wavered, and the handsome man in his early forties refused to let Savage's withering glare get to him.

It was the fourth pot in a row that Savage had won, which wasn't much considering he'd lost the eight previous ones between Tate and the other three men in the poker game. This hand, however, was different. This pot was upwards of one hundred dollars, and most of it was Tate's.

Savage had drifted into Concho Springs way station, Arizona Territory, the day before on a tired sorrel after three days of dodging Apaches. The town sat in the middle of desert country surrounded by giant saguaro cactus, prickly pear, ocotillo, and creosote bush. It was situated on a large spring which was its only water source. It was an oasis in a harsh land.

While out on the trail, Savage had come across an upturned stage. All of the six-up horse team was gone, and the driver, messenger, and passengers were dead. Every one of them had been scalped. The buzzards had done the rest.

He'd been told that it was the work of Rios and his Apache renegades. They were a small band of outcasts led by a half-breed. They stole everything they required to live and murdered anyone who stood in their way. Even their own kind wanted no part of them.

'Tread softly, Savage,' a new voice warned. 'He has a reputation.'

The man who'd spoken was a cavalry lieutenant by the name of Joel Porter. He was a slim man with dark hair and three days' growth of beard on his face. He led a patrol that was using the station as a stopover for the night. While most of his men were outside, both he and his sergeant were inside.

The lieutenant's words were true enough. Tate had a reputation as fast with a gun, a killer, a gambler, and a man not to be trifled with. Once on his wrong side, there was no turning back.

'Just go ahead and shoot the cheatin''

son of a bitch, Ned,' an attractive dark-haired woman in her late thirties urged Tate.

Tate nodded. 'I might just do that, Glory darlin'.'

Gloria Tate was Ned's wife. It was said that she was as bad as her husband. Rumor had it that she'd knifed a man outside of a saloon in New Mexico one night, just to take back the winnings her husband had lost. It couldn't be proved, however, and nothing was ever done about it.

Still seated in his chair, Savage turned his steely gaze upon Gloria. 'Ma'am, if I was you, I'd be tryin' to save my husband's life instead of tryin' to get him killed. Now if you ain't gonna do that, then the least you can do is to shut your damned mouth.'

The last words that spilled from his lips were harsh and filled with menace.

Gloria's jaw dropped and her eyes grew wide, unused to being spoken to in that manner. She looked to her husband. 'Are you gonna let him talk to me that way?' she screeched. 'Shoot him! Do it now, damn it!'

With the sound of his wife's cries still ringing in his ears, Tate went for the six-gun on his right thigh. It had only just cleared leather when Savage's .44 caliber Remington roared from beneath the table.

The slug punched through the tabletop and buried itself into the gambler's chest. His mouth hung open with the shock of its sudden impact. Tate remained on his feet, however, and fought to bring his six-gun up.

Savage rose, coming to his full height of six foot one. With a wisp of gunsmoke still rising from the barrel of the Remington, he brought it up, cocked the hammer and aimed at Tate.

'I told you your mouth was likely to get you killed,' he rasped, and pulled the trigger.

The bullet smashed into Tate's wide-open mouth. On the way in, it shattered his bottom teeth and deflected upwards. It blew out the back of his skull in a crimson spray of brains and bone fragments. Tate's six-gun fell from his lifeless fingers and clattered to the rough floorboards. His corpse followed it with a dull thud.

'Ned!' Gloria screamed. 'You murderin' bastard, you've killed him!'

Seemingly from nowhere, Gloria Tate drew a small knife with a double-edged blade. She raised it above her head and moved swiftly towards Savage. The polished steel glinted as it reflected the dim lantern light within the station. Gloria screamed bloody murder as she made to bring a death blow down upon her husband's killer.

Without a second thought, Savage's left hand balled into a fist and deftly clipped her on her petite chin when she came within reach. Gloria's screams ceased immediately and the knife fell from her grasp. Her knees went weak and as she collapsed, Savage caught her up and placed her limp body in the chair he'd been sitting in.

'Why didn't you put a bullet in the

stupid bitch's head too?' an older, unkempt prospector cackled from over at the small roughly built bar.

Savage gave him a look of disgust and was about to reply when there was movement at the station's front door as it swung open. A man in his late thirties entered. He was dressed in black and had a muscular build, tanned face, and saddlebags over his shoulder. He took in the scene before him, the dead body on the floor and the rest of the people in the room, before he said in a heavy southern drawl, 'Hell, did I miss somethin'?'

His name was Lucifer. The single-word title was all he needed, as it was a name everyone present knew. Lucifer was a killer for hire; a product of the war who, like many others, returned home to nothing and made a living any way he could. The cause of his current presence at Concho Springs was any-one's guess.

When the half-drunk prospector proudly told what he'd witnessed,

Lucifer looked across at Savage and said, 'Is that right? Seems to me I've heard of you, Savage. Ex-cavalry captain who killed a heap of fellers that did for your wife.'

All heads turned to stare at Savage, who was now seated at a different table with a mug of coffee in front of him.

'Don't believe all you hear,' he advised Lucifer.

'Sounds like good advice.' Lucifer smiled.

'He's a damned murderer is what he is,' the now conscious Gloria snarled.

'I'll take these for you, Mr. Lucifer,' the station manager, Bill Davis, offered, reaching for the saddlebags. 'I'll put them somewheres out of the way.'

Lucifer gave the rail-thin manager a cold look and said with menace, 'If anyone touches my saddlebags, I'll kill them.'

Davis withdrew his hand as though burned, fear etched on his face. Tension hung heavily in the room and was only broken when Lucifer smiled and said,

'Just kiddin'. Thank you, but I'll take care of them myself.'

Davis smiled nervously and walked back to the bar.

After a few more minutes, Porter and his sergeant left the room to head outside. Meanwhile, Lucifer found himself a table with a watered-down bottle of whiskey. Every now and then he looked up at Savage, sizing him up.

Savage decided enough was enough and got up from his seat and walked out. He stood in the center of the hard-packed yard and looked about. The sun had begun to sink and cast an orange hue across the desert. Large rock formations changed color, as did the cloudless sky. Later, once the sun was gone, it would cool down and the night air would take on a sharp bite.

The yard was deserted, but he headed around to the rear of the station where the cavalry troop was camped.

Porter and his solidly built sergeant were in a discussion about posting sentries when Savage showed. The sergeant saluted, then left the two of them to talk in private.

'Is there something I can do for you, Captain Savage?' Porter asked.

'Savage is just fine, Lieutenant,' Savage told him. 'I ain't a troop commander any more.'

Porter nodded. 'Fair enough. So is there anything I can help you with?'

'I was wondering if I could ride along with you fellers tomorrow. You know, safety in numbers, what with the Yavapai stirred up of late as well as that Rios feller thrown into the mix.'

'But we're only goin' back to Fort Craig tomorrow,' Porter pointed out. 'Is that the way you're headed?'

Craig was only another twenty miles to the north and had first been established in 1863 to protect travelers from the Apaches who lived in the Gila River and Salt River Valleys.

'It'll do,' Savage answered. 'I ain't got nowhere special to be.'

Porter thought for a moment, then nodded. 'It may be best. When we arrive, you can report to the colonel and tell him about the stage you found.'

'I guess I can do that,' Savage allowed. 'But what makes you so sure that it was Rios that hit the stage and not the Yavapai?'

'We ran across Rios in that area two days back,' Porter told him. 'We chased him for ten miles before we lost him. I'd say he doubled back and waited for the stage. It's not the first time that it's happened. Besides, the Yavapai have been stickin' to the mountains east of here lately and have caused no trouble.'

'That ain't what I saw the last three days,' Savage disagreed.

Suddenly there were shouts from inside the way station, followed by the sound of a gunshot.

2

Savage and Porter looked at each other and started to run towards the front of the building.

'Sergeant Russell, on me,' Porter shouted.

Russell began to follow, collecting another two other troopers along the way. When Savage and Porter burst through the front door, they found Lucifer standing over the body of the prospector, a Colt Navy Model .36 still in his hand. The old man lay on his back with a hole in his chest, a pool of blood starting to form.

Lucifer looked over at them and said nonchalantly, 'I gave fair warnin'. He was goin' through my saddlebags.'

Savage looked at him in disgust. 'I hope whatever he saw was worth dyin' over.'

'I think we need to have a look,'

Porter said aloud.

Lucifer shook his head. 'Nope, you don't.'

'Sergeant Russell,' Porter snapped.

The sergeant and the two troopers started forward, and Lucifer brought up his six-gun and thumbed back the hammer. They paused and looked questioningly at Porter.

'Just tell them to come ahead if you want them killed, soldier boy,' Lucifer sneered.

The lieutenant thought briefly, then said reluctantly, 'Stand down, Russell.'

The three cavalrymen backed off, and Lucifer smiled. 'There, that's better. Ain't no one likely to get killed now.'

He holstered his six-gun, and as soon as he did, Savage drew his Remington and thumbed back the hammer. The dry triple-click took everyone by surprise, Lucifer especially.

'Are you aimin' to use that?' he asked Savage.

'Only if I have to,' Savage informed him. 'The others may have stood down, but I ain't. Now let's see what is in those saddlebags of yours, and we'll know whether or not it was worth killin' for. Have a look, Sergeant Russell.'

Russell took the saddlebags and opened one side. He hissed loudly and threw them at Lucifer, who only just managed to catch them.

'You murderin' son of a bitch,' Russell snarled.

'What did you find, Sergeant?' Porter asked.

Russell turned and faced Porter, a look of revulsion on his face. 'The bastard has scalps in them, Lieutenant,' Russell reported. 'Apache scalps. The son of a bitch is scalp huntin'.'

'There is nothin' illegal about it,' Lucifer declared.

'There's nothing right about it either,' Porter snapped.

Savage stood and stared at the killer, and it took a deal of willpower not to let the hammer drop on the Remington. Instead, he motioned towards the door. 'Saddle your horse and get the hell out of here. Don't come back.'

Lucifer's eyes turned icy. 'You're a big man with that six-gun in your fist,' he hissed.

'And you'll be a dead one if you don't get the hell gone,' Savage snarled. 'Right now it's takin' all I have not to drop you where you stand. Now go!'

Lucifer saw the look in Savage's eyes, knew that he was a hair's breadth away from dying, and decided not to push things any further. He picked up the saddlebags and headed towards the door.

When the door closed, Savage holstered the Remington, looked across at Porter and said, 'I'd say that is why I've been seein' all them Yavapai the last few days. I reckon they're lookin' for that son of a bitch.'

Porter nodded. 'I agree.'

⋆   ⋆   ⋆

Lucifer was adjusting the saddle on his chestnut when Gloria Tate found him.

He was out by the corral in the dark preparing to leave when he heard the soft footfalls come up behind him.

Without turning he asked, 'Is there somethin' you wanted, ma'am?'

'I want to hire you,' Gloria Tate said. 'I want you to kill Savage for me.'

'No.'

'I'll pay you five hundred dollars. It is all I have.'

'I have a job.

'Killin' Indians for bounty?'

'It pays.'

'So you won't do it?'

'No.'

She watched as he mounted and rode off into the darkness, then called after him, 'Damn you!'

★　★　★

Twenty mounted troopers sat saddle, waiting for the order to move out. Horses stamped at the hard-packed earth, and the jingle of metal tack rang out in the still morning air. There remained a faint chill which would be gone as the sun climbed higher over the distant mountains and warmed the desert with its baking heat.

Savage saddled the sorrel and led the animal over to join the column.

'Are you ready to go?'

Savage nodded. 'Yeah. Have you seen our friend up on the ridge this mornin'?'

Porter looked to the east and saw the lone figure sitting atop a horse between two large saguaro plants. He sat motionless, staring out across the Concho Springs station at everything that happened.

'Do you think he's lookin' for Lucifer?' Porter asked.

'More than likely,' Savage said. 'Then again, he might be scoutin' the way station.'

Porter was about to send a couple of troopers out to the ridge, but before he could make the order, the Apache was gone.

'Oh well, let's go then.'

Five minutes later, amid the cacophony of hoof beats, the cavalry patrol plus one rode out of Concho Springs. If Porter had sent the troopers out to the ridge, they would've found more than one lone Apache. On the backside of the ridge, there were fifty.

★　★　★

The young trooper's shrill screams rang out as the razor-sharp blade bit into the flesh of his forehead below the hairline. As it was dragged across from left to right, the skin peeled back and left a flood of scarlet to cascade down his face, blinding him as it washed into his eyes.

Rios smiled viciously, showing yellowed teeth as he continued his bloody work. Two of his renegades held the young trooper still, their powerful sun-bronzed arms rippling as their muscles flexed against the struggles. There was a sickening sucking sound as Rios ripped the young man's scalp from his head, bringing forth an even louder wail of pain. Stepping back, Rios admired his work and thought about what to do next.

Rios was a 30-year-old half-Mexican half-Chiricahua Apache. He stood five feet ten inches tall and had a slim frame covered in whipcord muscle. His facial features came from his father's people, the Apache. From his mother's Mexican heritage he got his fiery temper. He wore a sleeveless cotton shirt, a breech cloth, and knee-high moccasins.

Suddenly Rios stepped forward and deftly stabbed the young man in the left eye with the point of his knife, not deep enough to kill but definitely enough to do some serious damage. The eye popped and a clear jelly-like substance oozed out of the ruined orb. This action brought about more screaming, though the sound was quite ragged as his throat was raw.

Rios had been lucky over the past two days, first with the stage and now here in the mountains, where he'd come across the young trooper. Behind him, seven of his renegade band watched on, enjoying the spectacle. But none more so than Rios.

The smell of hot urine wafted up as the captive's bladder released its contents and a pool formed, albeit briefly, between his legs. Rios wrinkled his nose in disgust. 'You piss yourself like a baby, white-eyes dog. You will go to your maker as a woman in his eyes.'

The knife flashed in the bright sunlight once more as Rios used it to slice open the front of the trooper's bloody tunic and the shirt beneath. A thin red line appeared against the young man's pale torso as a trickle of blood started where the finely honed blade had touched skin.

Rios looked about and motioned to a renegade who answered to the name Delgado. The bronzed warrior stepped forward and held out a thin cactus spine to the renegade leader, who took it and turned back to face the trooper.

Rios slid the spine into the flesh of

the trooper's middle, extracting another cry of intense pain. He turned back and took another two and did the same again. The fourth and fifth spines went into his face, while the next went into the trooper's remaining eye. The spine drew the same outcome on the gelatinous mass as the knife had on the other.

The torture continued for half an hour more before Rios grew bored and opened the young man's throat to watch him bleed out. They departed the gruesome scene and left him where he lay for the buzzards and other scavengers to pick his bones clean. Those not carted off would be all that remained, along with the uniform that he wore. The uniform of the Confederate States of America.

3

Fort Craig sat on a flat piece of ground not far from the Verde River. Most buildings in the small settlement were of adobe and brick construction. The exception was the main headquarters building, which was all timber.

At the center of the hard-packed earthen parade ground stood a flagpole which usually flew a large flag. By the time the patrol arrived back at the fort, Retreat had been blown and the flag had been neatly folded and put away ready for the following morning.

A glowing red sunset had turned the harsh Arizona landscape a spectacular myriad of colors by the time the patrol thundered into the fort. Savage stabled the sorrel with the rest of the cavalry mounts while Porter made his report to his commanding officer, Maxwell Travis. Travis looked to be middle-aged, with graying hair and a weathered face. He seemed imposing but only stood around six feet tall.

'From what I've heard, Colonel, he could be the answer to our problems.'

There was a look of concern on Travis's face, his deep-set green eyes hard to read. 'You could be right, Joel, although I don't much like the idea of how to accomplish getting him on our side.'

'It may be the only way.'

Nodding, Travis said, 'OK, go and get him.'

Porter found Savage just as he was finishing with his horse. 'The colonel wants to see you.'

Savage nodded. 'Let's go, then.'

Savage followed Porter across to the headquarters building and entered to find Travis waiting patiently.

'Pleased to meet you, Mr. Savage,' Colonel Maxwell Travis greeted him with an outstretched hand.

'You too, Colonel,' Savage said, taking it firmly.

Travis motioned to a timber chair. 'Take a seat.'

Savage sat down and waited for Travis to do the same.

The office was quite large and the lamp on Travis's battered desk kept it well lit. There was a potbellied stove in the corner with a coffee pot simmering on it and a small bucket beside it which held a stock of wood.

'The lieutenant told me about the stage you came across,' Travis stated. 'Care to tell me about it?'

Savage relayed the information about what he'd found, and when he was finished, Travis sat silently as he mulled it all over. He looked across at Porter, who'd remained after showing Savage into the office.

'I think you may be right, Joel,' Travis conceded.

'Yes, sir.'

Travis turned his gaze back to Savage. 'Mr. Savage, I have a proposition for you. I'll tell you straight up that you are not going to like it, but it is something that needs to be done. From what I've heard about you, we believe that you could be the man to accomplish it.'

Savage was immediately wary and asked cautiously, 'What would that be?'

'I would like to commission you to hunt down the killer known as Rios, and his renegades,' Travis told him.

'You what?' Savage asked, not sure he'd heard right.

'It's a job for one man,' Travis went on. He held up a hand when Savage made to protest. 'I know what you're going to say. That there are too many of them and that it should be a job for the army. And you're probably right. But if I take or send a troop into the mountains where he usually retreats to, he'll see them coming from a mile away and run. One man will have a better chance to get close without being detected. The other reason is that if the Apache are out of the mountains causing trouble, as you seem to think due to this Lucifer fellow, then I'll need every man here at the fort. I'll pay you for your troubles, Mr. Savage. A sum of two hundred dollars.'

'No you won't, Travis,' Savage said with finality. 'I ain't goin'.'

Travis stared at Savage, unblinking. 'Is there any way that you could be persuaded to go, Mr. Savage?'

'No.'

Travis nodded thoughtfully. 'I was afraid of that.'

Savage looked questioningly at Travis, who shifted his gaze across to Porter.

'Bring in the sergeant-major.'

Porter opened the door and called out an order. The man who approached wasn't alone. Accompanying the burly sergeant-major were three well-armed men. Savage was immediately on edge.

'Sergeant-Major Thomas, arrest Mr. Savage and lock him in the guard house,' Travis ordered. 'We'll hold him there until the proper authorities can be notified.'

Savage bolted from his seat as the

four men made for him. He dropped his hand to the Remington at his side and stared wide-eyed at Travis. 'The hell you're arrestin' me.'

'I'm sorry, Mr. Savage,' Travis apologized. 'But when you murder an unarmed man, you leave me no choice.'

'What the hell are you talkin' about?' Savage asked, flabbergasted. 'I didn't shoot no unarmed man.'

'No? What about the man at Concho Springs?'

'He had a . . . ' Realization dawned on Savage as to what the Fort Craig Commander was up to. 'Hell, I see what you're gettin' at. No way. You can't do it.'

'But I can,' Travis informed him. 'I have at least one witness who will attest that is what happened.'

'What about the others who were there?'

'I don't care about them. I care about all the people who will continue to die if that bastard is not stopped.'

'What if I can't get him?'

'I have a feeling that once you start something, you won't stop until it's finished.'

Savage shook his head. He'd been forced to kill before, and it looked as though he was about to ride down that trail again. One of death and violence.

'All right, I'll do it.'

Travis smiled as though nothing had happened. 'Good. I knew you'd see it our way.'

★ ★ ★

Shortly after midnight, Savage was shaken awake by Porter. 'What is it?'

'Come over to headquarters,' Porter ordered grimly. 'A rider just came in. Concho Springs is gone.'

Savage hurried to dress and followed Porter. When he walked into the office, he saw one of the men he'd played cards with. Blood-stained and torn clothing hung from his wounded body.

'It seems you were right, Mr. Savage,' Travis informed him. 'A large bunch of

Apaches hit the Concho Springs way station shortly after you all rode out yesterday. Mr. Rivers here is all that's left, albeit injured.'

Rivers turned to Savage. 'It was bad. Everyone was killed by them, men and women. I was only left alive so I could carry a message here to the fort.'

'What message?' Savage asked.

It was Travis who spoke again. 'They want the man who killed some of their own and took their scalps. They'll continue to make war until he is given to them.'

Rivers's grubby face screwed up into a mask of hatred. 'That damn son of a bitch Lucifer did this. He caused it all. I hope them Apache catch up to him and kill him slow. It's all the bastard deserves.'

'It seems you'll have your hands full with the Yavapai-Apache for a while,' Savage pointed out.

Rivers shook his head vigorously. 'No. It weren't Yavapai that done it. They was Chiricahua.'

Travis nodded grimly. 'Thank you, Mr. Rivers. If you'd care to wait out in the other room, once we finish here I'll have Lieutenant Porter find you somewhere to sleep.'

Rivers nodded his thanks and left the room.

'It looks as though the situation has become more complex than we first thought,' Travis observed.

Savage shook his head in disbelief. 'This just keeps on getting better. Next thing you'll be wantin' me to round up them Chiricahuas for you.'

Travis let the sarcasm pass. 'I'll have patrols sent out to see if we can find them.'

Savage turned and started to walk out.

'Where are you going?'

'Back to bed,' Savage informed him without turning around. 'With all this work I have to do for the U.S. Cavalry, I'm gonna need my sleep.'

4

After two days, Savage hadn't made it very far, with most of his time taken up trying to stay alive by avoiding Apaches. He was in mountainous desert country: a wilderness of saguaro, prickly pear, and other cacti, and of cholla, ocotillo, and acacia along the washes.

And while it was desert, there were still creeks along the deeper canyons. The previous evening, as the setting sun cast its magical purple pall over the surrounding desert, Savage heard a mountain lion's roar echo from the surrounding craggy peaks, beautiful and deadly at the same time.

He now bent down to fill his canteen in the stream. When it was full, he stood and replaced the cap. He felt like a lost soul with no direction, wandering the mountains trying to locate a man who didn't want to be found; and he had no idea where he was holed up.

Suddenly the sorrel stopped drinking and lifted its head. Its ears pricked, and it looked back towards a rock-and-cactus-covered slope. Savage dropped his hand to the butt of the Remington and casually walked over and looped the canteen's leather strap about the saddle horn.

While he did this, his eyes roved constantly over the slope, and he scanned the ridge line. It seemed to be clear, though anyone could be hiding out there amongst the rocks.

Savage fidgeted some more with his saddle, careful to keep the horse between himself and the ridge, and he continued to search out the source of his angst. Still nothing. There were at least two more hours before dark, so Savage climbed back into the saddle and kept on with his blind search.

★ ★ ★

Lucifer lay motionless in silence as he watched Savage disappear. For a brief moment he thought his presence had been detected; but when Savage had mounted and ridden off, he breathed a sigh of relief that all was good.

'Now what would you be doin' out here?' he wondered aloud.

Then he thought back to the incident at the way station and how Savage had made him look a fool. Anger surged through him as the scene played out in his mind.

'I think we just might have to find out what it is,' he muttered again.

★ ★ ★

By luck, Savage cut the trail of Rios and his renegades in a wash the next morning. At least he hoped it was them, but wouldn't be able to tell until he got close enough to see. It took several more hours of careful tracking before he could confirm that he was finally on their tail.

They were stopped in a canyon with a small stream flowing through it. Savage heard them well before he laid eyes on them. Or rather he heard the blood-curdling screams of the man they were having *fun* with.

Savage eased the sorrel off what passed as a trail and hid it out of sight in a dry wash. Next, he took the Yellow Boy from its saddle scabbard and circled around to climb a low hill to get a better view. He lay belly down between two rocks so he had a clear field of vision the 150 yards to where the group of renegades worked on their captive. What he saw made his stomach turn.

Rios and his men had a lone figure strapped down on the only large flat-topped rock for miles. The man's clothes were torn to shreds, and they were busy working on him with knives that glinted in the bright sunlight.

Savage ground his teeth absentmindedly as he watched, his anger boiling just below the surface. A thin sheen of sweat broke out across his face as he restrained himself from acting rashly, but he could virtually feel the tortured man's pain.

'Enough is enough, you sons of bitches,' Savage cursed, and slid the Yellow Boy forward.

Another howl of pain filled the air, which was followed by shouts of excitement. One of the renegades held up something above his head and Savage realized that it was the man's scalp.

Savage sighted down the barrel of the Yellow Boy and squeezed the trigger. The report of the rifle cracked in the air, and the renegade who held the grisly prize aloft died as his head seemed to explode when the .44 caliber slug smashed into it.

Levering in a new round, Savage shifted his aim and brought down another renegade. This time the bullet punched into the killer's chest and blew out his back in a bright spray of crimson.

Cries of alarm sounded as a wave of panic swept through the survivors. Savage's gun spat once more and yet another went down.

The remaining renegades, Rios included, scattered amongst the brush and rocks and began to return fire. Bullets started to pepper the two rocks beside him, so Savage slid back down the slope to change position.

More shots peppered where he'd been, and the tell-tale sign of gunsmoke gave Savage an accurate location for each of the remaining renegades. Savage fired at a flash of color amongst some acacia and saw the slug snap off a branch then whine harmlessly away off an unseen rock.

One of the renegades broke cover, and Savage fired two fast shots in his direction. Both missed, and his target dropped behind a clump of brush. Another broke cover and this time, Savage's accuracy knocked the attacker sprawling in the dirt.

Four down.

Things started to change with an almost rehearsed precision as the remaining renegades started moving from cover to cover in short bursts, giving Savage almost no chance of a sure shot. With every shot that he missed, the closer they got to him.

He reloaded and fired off three more rounds at the fast-moving targets, almost certain that he'd hit at least one more of the renegades. It wasn't good enough. There were still five more out there amongst the rocks and brush.

Suddenly, from out of nowhere another rifle opened up on the right. There were cries of alarm from the renegades, and Savage watched as they started to scatter.

Standing up, he worked the lever of his rifle and kept up a steady rate of fire. Before the renegades could reach their horses, three more were down. The two remaining ones leaped upon the backs of the closest mounts and kicked them brutally into motion.

Two more shots rang out from the

unknown shooter, and one of the remaining renegades fell from a fast-moving horse. One rider remained, but no amount of shot could bring him down and he got away.

'Damn it,' Savage cursed. He hoped that the rider who'd managed to flee wasn't Rios.

He moved down the slope towards the scene of the carnage. The first two renegades he encountered were dead. He carried on, and a flicker of movement caught his eye.

Savage palmed up the Remington with blinding speed. By the time it came level, the hammer was thumbed all the way back and ready to fire.

'Whoa, hold on there,' Lucifer announced, causing Savage to stop short of pulling the trigger. 'I ain't tryin' to kill you. If anythin', I saved your hair.'

'What the hell are you doin' here?' Savage snapped, noting how the killer held his Henry rifle at the ready.

'Is that any way to speak to a man

who just pulled your chestnuts out of the fire?' he asked icily.

Savage said nothing. A wounded renegade moaned from the ground between them and attracted his attention. Before he could move, Lucifer had raised his rifle and shot the man dead.

Savage's gaze snapped back to Lucifer, who lowered the Henry as a thin stream of gunsmoke rose from the barrel. He shrugged his shoulders. 'What? He's safer that way.'

'What's next?' Savage snarled. 'Are you gonna take their scalps?'

Lucifer smiled. 'I didn't think of that. Thanks.'

'You touch any one of them and I'll kill you.' The menace in Savage's voice was unmistakable.

Lucifer's smile vanished. 'You'll try.'

Savage ignored the comment and approached the figure tied to the rock. Mercifully, death had claimed him. It looked as though a stray bullet had finished him off. What concerned

Savage most was the dead man's clothing.

'What are you doin' all the way out here, anyhow?' Lucifer asked, interrupting Savage's thoughts.

Savage moved away from the corpse and looked around at the dead renegades. 'My business.'

Lucifer watched him thoughtfully. 'He's not here.'

'Who?'

'Rios,' Lucifer answered. 'It was him that got away.'

Savage cursed silently under his breath, but the expression on his face gave it away.

'So it was him you were after,' Lucifer scoffed.

Once more, Savage ignored him. He walked back to the man draped across the rock and said to Lucifer, 'Come over here and tell me what you find strange about this dead feller.'

Lucifer frowned and did as he was asked. He stood beside Savage and looked down at the bloodied corpse.

After a period of silence, Lucifer said, 'The only thing I can see is that he's wearin' a Reb uniform. But that ain't uncommon. After the war, that's all some folks had left to wear.'

Savage nodded. 'True. I take it you served the Southern cause?'

Lucifer's jaw set firm. 'I did.'

'Well take a close look at the uniform he's wearin', beyond the blood and everythin' else, and tell me what you see.'

Frowning, Lucifer studied the clothing once more; then his face changed when he saw it. He shook his head in bewilderment and looked across at Savage. 'Christ almighty,' he said in a low voice. 'He's meant to be in Mexico. What's he doin' here?'

'If you gentlemen would be so kind as to put your weapons down, I would much appreciate it,' a deep Southern drawl sounded from behind them.

Both men whirled to see who'd spoken and were surprised to see not one man standing there, but eight.

Eight armed men had materialized from the surrounding desert, all dressed in Confederate uniforms. Their leader, a solidly built man who stood a shade under six feet, wore sergeant's chevrons on his sleeve.

'Haven't you heard, Sergeant?' Savage asked. 'The war is over.'

'The war will never be over for us,' the man snapped, then spat in the sand at his feet to emphasize his point.

'Hey lookee there, Esa,' a thin corporal pointed out. 'That feller there is wearin' Yankee blue britches.'

Savage figured Esa to be in his early thirties. His brown hair was shaggy atop a rugged face.

'Get their guns, Colter,' Esa ordered.

'Sure thing, Sergeant Brown.'

Colter moved forward and relieved them of their weapons, all the while smiling like an idiot, exposing blackened teeth.

'Hey, you don't have to take mine,' Lucifer protested. 'I'm on your side.'

'I guess we'll find out, won't we?' Esa

sneered. 'Get them on their horses. We'll take them to see the major.'

'Don't you mean the general?' another trooper asked.

'No, I don't.'

One of the other troopers had checked out the man on the rock. 'He's dead, Esa.'

'Two in a matter of days.' Esa nodded grimly. Then he looked at Savage and Lucifer. 'Well, at least you two got them.'

'One got away,' Savage admitted. 'Rios.'

'Shame you didn't get the son of a bitch.'

Esa was about to say more when a trooper came bounding up to them. 'We gotta ride, Esa,' he said hurriedly. 'All them gunshots have drawn some attention.'

'All right, let's go,' Esa snapped. 'Mount up. We got company.'

A trooper brought forward the horses of Savage and Lucifer. They clambered into their saddles before being caught up by a wave of their captors on the trail, riding hard and deeper into the mountains.

5

An hour later, the small band of riders crested a ridge. Savage noticed a man who sat at the top of a small rock wall they passed: a sentry. Then they dropped down into a sandy valley with copper-colored cliffs on both sides. The scarred bluffs seemed to sprout from the desert floor. The valley was filled with giant saguaros and prickly pear. Scattered across the floor were lots of small desert shrubs no higher than a man. It was a harsh landscape that greeted them, but the one thing that Savage noticed was that it did have water. A small stream fed through the valley, giving an almost constant supply.

Then Savage saw a small clump of adobe buildings in the distance. Their copper color helped blend them into the surrounding landscape, and a cursory glance would easily miss them. It was only a small settlement.

The pace of the horses dropped back as they neared the buildings, and Savage could make out a parade ground and a flagpole that flew the Confederate battle flag.

'What the hell is this place?' Savage asked a trooper next to him.

'Fort Jackson,' he said proudly. 'Named after the second best general the Confederacy ever had.'

Knowing the answer before the question ever passed his lips, Savage asked, 'Who was the best?'

'General Joseph Orville Shelby,' the trooper said. Then he added, 'Our commanding officer.'

'Shut your yap, Wade,' Esa barked.

When the riders eased their mounts to a stop on the parade ground, more Confederate cavalrymen started to gather, causing a stir. Savage figured there to be around two hundred men in the fort at his best estimate.

Before they could dismount, the

group was approached by a captain with dark hair and solid build. Savage put his age at around middle thirties and his height at about six feet.

'What do we have here, Sergeant?' he asked.

Esa gave him a look of disdain. 'Prisoners, Captain Simeon. We found them while we were searching for Mendelson.'

'And?'

'Mendelson is dead.'

Simeon shook his head. 'Too bad. Where are you taking them?'

'To see Major Perkins.'

'Sir.'

'Sir.'

Simeon stared at them thoughtfully, then nodded. 'Carry on.'

Savage watched Simeon walk away and couldn't fight the feeling snagged in his mind that something wasn't right with Fort Jackson.

★   ★   ★

Major Christopher Perkins stood near his roughly built plank desk and stared intently at the two men, trying to decide what to do with them. Not that there was much of a decision to make. They couldn't be let go, so would have to be treated as spies and dealt with accordingly. Perkins was a square-jawed medium-built man with brown hair and gray eyes, and Savage put his age somewhere in the vicinity of forty.

Savage looked about the room. It was sparsely furnished, having only an open fire for warmth, the major's desk and two chairs, one of which now contained Perkins. When they had first arrived in front of the major, Lucifer had quickly stated that he was no threat, though Perkins would have none of it.

'I'll thank you to shut up,' Perkins ordered. 'I've listened to enough of your squawk. If I hear any more of it, I'll have Esa gag you.'

A dark cloud descended on Lucifer's face, but he remained silent. Something else seemed to settle in the killer's expression too. Something unreadable that Savage couldn't quite fathom.

'Nice set-up you all have here, Perkins,' Savage stated.

Perkins dragged his lingering gaze from Lucifer and looked over at Savage. 'That's Major Perkins to you,' he ordered.

Savage ignored the directive. 'How long have you fellers been out here?'

'I'll ask the questions, damn it!' Perkins snapped.

This is going well, Savage thought. 'OK.'

'What are you two men doing here in these mountains?'

'I don't know about him,' Savage said, pointing at Lucifer, 'but I'm here huntin' a feller for the army.'

A look of alarm flitted across Perkins's face. When he spoke, a trace of it was evident in his voice. 'Who?' he asked urgently, concerned that they would be discovered.

'A feller called Rios,' Savage explained. 'The same one who killed your man out in the desert west of here.'

Perkins's eyes snapped to Esa, who nodded. 'They were engaged with the hostiles when we came upon them.'

'Thanks for your help,' Lucifer said drily.

Esa's gaze hardened as he stared at Lucifer, but his discipline held sway so he wasn't drawn by the comment.

Suddenly the door opened and all heads turned to see two men walk in. One was Simeon and the other was General Jo Shelby.

'What can I do for you, General?' Perkins demanded.

Savage was taken aback by the manner in which the subordinate had addressed Shelby. When he'd served, it was unthinkable that one would speak in such a way to their commanding officer.

Shelby was in his middle thirties with dark wavy hair and a mustache and goatee. Beneath the facial hair were lines from years of the pressures of command. His uniform was a little loose on his now slim stature, another sign of hard times.

Shelby ignored Perkins and fixed his gaze upon Esa. 'Why weren't these men brought to me, Sergeant?' he snapped, his dark angry eyes burning holes in the man.

Then the second thing happened that convinced Savage that all was not right in Fort Jackson. Esa remained silent, almost openly defiant.

'Well?'

'Answer the general, Sergeant,' Simeon snarled.

'I had him bring them to me,' Perkins cut in. 'I didn't see the point in worrying you with such a trivial matter.'

'Arrogant bastard,' Simeon mumbled, but loud enough for Savage to hear.

'Take them away and lock them up, Ben,' Shelby ordered. 'I'll talk to them after.'

'Yes, sir.'

'Wait!' Perkins protested loudly. 'If you want to lock them up for the time being, then fine; but I suggest you treat that one as a spy and have him shot.'

Perkins was staring hard at Savage.

'Why, might I ask?' said Shelby.

'His britches are Yankee issue.'

'Hmmm,' Shelby said thoughtfully, carefully studying Savage. 'You did serve, I gather?'

Savage nodded. 'Cavalry. Captain.'

Shelby smiled. 'Good. Then you shall join me for our evening meal tonight. Take them away, Ben.'

Savage couldn't help but notice the smoldering rage in Perkins as he glared hostilely at Shelby. Yes, sir. There was definitely something wrong at Fort Jackson.

★ ★ ★

Two hours after the sun had gone down that evening and left a cold chill across the high desert, Simeon came for Savage. The solid timber door to the small cell in which Savage was sequestered opened and the captain entered.

'General Shelby is waiting.'

'Lead the way,' Savage told him.

They crossed the parade ground and entered an adobe building not much bigger than the one Perkins used. The room, however, was well lit and three meals had been laid out on a rickety table. They were served on tin plates but looked quite appetizing to Savage, having not eaten for most of the day.

'Welcome, Mr. Savage,' Shelby greeted him. 'Please take a seat. You too, Ben.'

'The food looks mighty good, General,' Savage observed.

'Antelope stew,' Shelby said. 'Nothing fancy, but good nonetheless.'

They ate in silence and once they'd finished, Savage said, 'Can I ask you somethin', General? It's merely a curiosity, but it's been naggin' me since we arrived.'

Shelby nodded. 'Please do.'

'Why aren't you in Mexico like everyone thinks? Accordin' to all reports, that's where you all went.'

Shelby smiled. 'Yes. Holed up in Mexico with a thousand men ready to make the South great again.'

Savage couldn't help but notice the sarcastic tone in the man's voice.

'All fanciful tales told by drunks and men who have no idea what they're talking about,' Shelby said, picking up a cup of coffee. He took a sip and continued. 'In reality, Mr. Savage, I rode into Mexico with no more than two hundred men, most of whom you would have seen when you arrived today. We were welcomed at first, but after a while we were treated as intruders in their country. The Mexican people became quite bitter towards us, so we left. And this is where we ended up.'

Shelby paused once more to sip his coffee, then stared silently across the rim at Savage before saying something that stunned him.

'Now I want to go home to Missouri.'

6

'Why are you tellin' me this?' Savage asked Shelby uncertainly.

'Because I need your help to do it, Mr. Savage,' Shelby explained. 'There are those among my men who believe that the Southern cause is everything and would not hesitate to kill anyone who stands against it. Even me.'

'Would that someone happen to be Major Perkins, by any chance?'

Shelby nodded. 'It would.'

'We should have shot the son of a bitch before it got this far,' Simeon spat vehemently. Then he gathered himself. 'Sorry, General.'

'I agree, Ben. We should have.'

'Why not now?'

'Because if something like that were to happen now, then the divisions between the men could tear wide apart and they might turn on each other. I've had enough of war and killing, Mr. Savage, and I want to go home. Many of them still hold blind hope that one day the South will again be great. Can you understand that?'

'I think so.'

'My thinking is that if you accept the task I wish to set you, then just maybe it'll save lives all around.'

'What is it that you want me to do?'

Shelby signaled to Simeon, who topped up Savage's mug with coffee. 'I want you to escape, and I want you to ride out of here to the nearest fort and report our presence to the commanding officer.'

'Is that all?'

'Yes.'

'I hate to tell you this, General, but won't a whole troop of cavalry arrivin' on your doorstep invite more killin'?'

'I'm hoping that if it happens, my refusal to fight might persuade them all to give up and go home.'

'I'm guessin' some of them ain't got homes to go to,' Savage suggested.

'That is the sad fact of it all, Mr. Savage,' Shelby allowed. 'But at least they'll all still be alive.'

'What about Perkins? Where does he fit in all of this?'

Shelby sighed. 'I'm afraid he's the wild card in the deck. He's up to something, but we don't know what.'

'Will you do it?' Simeon asked impatiently.

Savage glanced at him then back to Shelby. 'OK. How are you gonna pass off the escape?'

'Let me worry about that,' Shelby said. 'All you need to know is that Ben will come for you tonight and get you out.'

'What about Lucifer?' Savage said, wondering about the scalp hunter.

'He goes too. Can't have one of you escaping without the other. Is that a problem?'

Savage shook his head. 'Nope.'

'Then you leave tonight.'

★　★　★

'We're getting' outa here tonight,' Savage spoke to Lucifer in a low voice.

'Says who?' he shot back skeptically.

'Just be ready, damn it,' Savage whispered harshly. 'OK?'

It was just after midnight when Simeon came for them. Using the shadows, they were able to slip outside of the fort's perimeter. The moon was only quarter, so there wasn't much light.

Savage, Lucifer and Simeon were met on the outskirts of the fort by four other men who had their horses and weapons. Once mounted, they let the horses pick their way along the valley until they started the climb to the top of the ridge. Halfway up, Savage stopped.

'What's the matter?' Simeon asked, stopping his mount beside Savage.

'What about the lookout at the top?'

'You don't have to worry about that,' Simeon assured him. 'The sentry tonight was appointed by me.'

Once outside the valley, they stopped.

Savage sat saddle beside Simeon and said, 'It'll be at least six days before I return.'

'Not to worry,' Simeon replied. Once you're both reported dead, no one will give you a second thought.'

★　★　★

'Sir, Savage and the other one have escaped,' Esa informed Perkins the following morning.

'How?' Perkins asked in a low voice that dripped with rage.

'I don't know.'

'Has a party been sent out after them?'

Esa nodded. 'Captain Simeon took a small detail out.'

'Damn it,' Perkins cursed vehemently. 'Have some men organized and dressed in the Union uniforms we have. If they make it out of the mountains alive, he's going to bring trouble, so we need to have the plan together now.'

'I'll see to it, sir.'

Thirty minutes later, the door burst open and Shelby strode in. He glared at Perkins and asked harshly, 'What on earth are the men doing out there dressed like Union Cavalry troops? I demand to know now.'

'It is all a part of my plan to join forces with the Apaches,' Perkins explained. 'Have you ever heard the expression 'the enemy of my enemy is my friend'?'

Shelby nodded.

'Well, *General*, by the end of this day, the Yavapai Apaches will be crying out for the blood of the Union soldiers who killed their brothers. After which, I shall approach them and we'll discuss terms of an alliance. I'm about to double the size of our army, maybe even triple it, and then I'll take them into Texas and drive out the carpetbaggers, the Union supporters, and the soldiers. Once that's done, more will flock to the battle flag, and then we can start making the Confederacy whole again.'

Shelby noticed the distant look in

Perkins's eyes and shook his head in disbelief. 'You're insane,' he snorted. 'Do you really think the Apaches will join forces with you? All you'll succeed in doing is getting all my men killed.'

'*Your* men?' Perkins spat as his face took on a look of contempt. 'You dare to call them *your* men? They ceased being your men the day you lost the will to fight.'

'I still give the orders here, Perkins,' Shelby reminded him.

'Not anymore,' the major growled. 'You'll be put under arrest and tried for treason by a military court.'

Before Shelby could say anything else, Perkins had his six-gun out and cocked. Shelby stared at him coldly.

'You won't get away with this,' he snapped.

'We'll see.'

★   ★   ★

Shelby watched from the window of his cell as the dozen blue-clad men rode

61

out of Fort Jackson under the command of Perkins's lap-dog sergeant. He cursed loudly at his own stupidity. He should never have let it come to this. And now it looked as though his efforts of late to keep his men alive would amount to nothing, unless by some miracle his plan with Savage worked.

'General?' a voice interrupted his thoughts.

Shelby frowned, at first thinking he was hearing things.

'General Shelby?' This time it was louder.

Turning away from the window, he hurried across to the solid wooden door of the cell. 'Who's there?'

'Larry Granville, sir.'

'Are you alone, Sergeant Granville?'

'Yes, sir.'

Shelby paused for a moment. 'I need you to do something for me, Sergeant. I want you to find Captain Simeon.'

For the next couple of minutes, Shelby elaborated to Granville what he needed from him. 'Did you get all of that?'

'Yes, sir.'

'Good man. Now get it done. The lives of your compatriots depend on you.'

★   ★   ★

'How much longer do we have to sit out here in this damned heat, sir?' asked a gaunt-faced trooper.

'Until I say it's time to head back, Sloan. And not before,' Simeon answered.

'Do you think the general's plan will work?'

'I hope so, Sloan. We've all been away from home too long.'

'I ain't got a home,' Sloan said solemnly.

'Rider comin' in!' cried a trooper atop a rock outcrop.

The small band of men scrambled to scoop up weapons and take firing positions. They hid behind jagged lumps of rock and small tightly packed clumps of brush.

'It's Sergeant Granville, Captain.'

Simeon let out a relieved sigh and stood out in the open to greet the incoming man.

Granville brought his hard-blowing mount to a stop in front of Simeon and gasped, 'I'm glad you're still here, Captain. If you weren't, I don't know what I would have done.'

'What is it?' Simeon asked, seeing the concern on the sergeant's face.

Granville slid from the saddle and hurriedly filled Simeon in on the events happening at the fort.

'All right, let's get mounted and get the general out,' Simeon snapped angrily.

'Wait, sir,' Granville called after the retreating captain. 'The general said for you to hunt down Savage and warn him about what Perkins was up to.'

'But that means leaving him locked up.'

'I don't think he's worried about

that, sir. I think he's more worried about the men and what could happen if this crazy scheme of Perkins's works out.'

Simeon nodded. 'OK. The rest of you get your horses and go with Granville.'

★ ★ ★

From his position high up on the ridge, hidden from sight and the heat of the sun, a lone figure lay watching the events unfold below him. He watched as they separated, then waited until the larger group disappeared from sight. Then he stood up and slowly jogged down the backside of the slope to where his horse was tethered.

He unhitched the reins and launched himself gracefully onto the animal's back. Then he heeled it hard, forcing the animal to respond instantly. Once out from behind the ridge, Rios turned his horse to follow the lone rider.

★ ★ ★

Sergeant Esa Brown lay belly down next to a large saguaro that sat proudly on the small hill. He raised his field glasses and looked about the camp below him. He studied it carefully so he wouldn't miss anything. They wanted no surprises, and none of the Yavapai must be allowed to escape.

For five long minutes, he lay unmoving and watched them, the sun searing his exposed skin. And then he slithered back down the slope to where his men awaited him.

'It's time,' he told them. 'Remember, no one gets away.'

'Are there women and children amongst them, Esa?' asked one of the men.

'They're Indians, nothin' more,' Esa growled in a low voice. 'Don't hesitate. Kill them all.'

The riders divided into two groups. When they split, they closed in on the camp from both sides of the hill. By the time the Yavapai knew they were there, it was too late.

The first slug from Esa's six-gun punched a hole in an old man's head and left another much larger one when it blew out the back and scattered his brains across the desert.

Immediately the cries and screams started. Women wailed as they scooped up their children and tried to escape the killing zone. An Apache youth stood defiantly against the charging soldiers with an old rusted Dragoon pistol. He raised it up and pulled the trigger. A great blue-gray puff of smoke spewed forth from the barrel, hiding the boy's face.

A blue-clad trooper fired a shot from his sidearm and the boy crumpled, a red stain appearing on the bronzed skin of his chest. The trooper didn't stop at that. He aimed his horse at the prone form and rode over the top of the corpse, the horse's hard hoof pulping the head as it smashed through the rest of the shattered skull.

Esa dragged his horse to a stop in the middle of the camp and emptied his pistol at fleeing natives. While he reloaded, a young male emerged from nowhere and loosed an arrow that streaked through the air and buried itself into a trooper's throat. The gravely wounded man opened his mouth in shock and a strong flow of crimson ran unhindered from his maw before he fell from his horse.

Esa cursed and shifted his aim. The young Apache had raised his bow to loose another arrow when he was blown off his feet by a slug from Esa's gun.

A woman launched an attack upon another mounted trooper, armed with only a knife. She grabbed at his jacket and attempted to dislodge him from his horse. The trooper turned and raised his six-gun and took a swipe at her. He got her a glancing blow but she ignored it. He took another swipe for the same effect. Then he raised the six-gun for another blow when she drove her knife up into his armpit. The trooper's high-pitched scream rang throughout the camp and he dropped the six-gun into the desert sand.

'Damned bitch,' he shouted, spittle flying from his lips.

The woman wrenched the knife free and stabbed the trooper in the thigh, dragging it down and across. Warm blood spurted from the wound and covered her hand. She looked up into his pained face and spat at him.

'White-eye dog,' she screamed at him.

Seeing his plight, another blue-clad trooper rode up behind the snarling woman and blew her brains out of the front of her head.

'Are you OK?' the soldier shouted over the din.

The wounded soldier smiled wanly. Blood started to trickle from the corner of his mouth as the true effect of the first wound was revealed.

'She killed me,' he managed to gurgle before more blood spilled from his mouth and he toppled from the saddle.

Now two of the attackers were dead, and things were about to get worse.

A further cry of pain caused Esa to shift his gaze, and he saw another trooper with an arrow sticking from his midsection. He looked for the shooter and located him sitting atop a horse at the crest of a ridge not fifty yards away. A young man had drawn the string back on his bow to fire another arrow, but he wasn't alone. There were five others with him, all young men, all armed, and all of them were about to rain death upon the attackers.

'Look to your front!' Esa shouted above the din.

The Apaches loosed their arrows and two of Esa's troopers were hit. An arrow took the first man in his chest and the next buried deeply in the other's torso. The first man fell from the saddle and lay still in the desert sand. The second hunched over his saddle as the pain of his wound kicked in.

Five men were now out of action.

'Shoot the bastards on the hill!' Esa ordered as he snapped off a shot in the Apache's direction.

A fusillade of gunfire rattled out, and Esa saw one of the warriors knocked back with a red bloom on his torso. The others, however, were unmoved and fired another volley at the troopers.

There was a high-pitched human-like scream as a horse took an arrow in its muscular neck. It staggered about and its rider fought to keep it upright. Every breath that blew out of its nostrils sent a fine mist of blood into the air until it lost the battle and slumped onto its side. The rider spilled into the sand, pinned by his leg.

'Esa! Esa, help!' he screamed as fear of being left there gripped him.

'Damn it to hell!' Esa shouted loudly. 'Somebody pick up Croft. We're gettin' outa here.'

But it was too late, as a younger Apache woman emerged from the brush and produced a razor-sharp knife and slashed the unsuspecting trooper's throat. Blood sprayed bright and hot, and a shuddering spasm rippled through him as he died.

The trooper who'd been about to help him raised a gun and fired at the young woman. The sand kicked up at her feet and she darted away behind a clump of brush before a second shot could be fired.

Upon the crest, another Apache died with two slugs in him, which only served to anger his companions; and their renewed war cries rang out clearly above the chaos.

'Come on, let's go!' Esa shouted, heeling his mount savagely.

Behind him, his remaining men followed, including the two wounded men who were held in the saddle by the riders beside them. They were a mile from the Apache camp when a trooper named Smith called out to Esa to slow down. They eased the horses back to a walk, then stopped.

'We can't keep goin' like this, Esa,' Smith warned him. 'Not with Wilson and Brown in this condition.'

Esa looked at his shrunken band. He'd left four men dead in the Apache camp and now he had two more in bad shape. He moved his horse around so he could look at the wounded.

Wilson had the broken shaft of an arrow sticking from his belly. Esa shook his head. Wilson was as good as dead. He just hadn't lain down yet. The other man, Brown, had an arrow sticking out of his torso. He was in pain, but looked to be in better shape than Wilson.

Esa casually reached out and snapped the arrow off as close to Brown's body as possible. Brown bit back a curse at the rough treatment.

'We'll dig that arrow head outa you when we get back,' he told him.

He looked over at Wilson. The man was hunched over as a fiery pain coursed through his middle. Nothing could be done for him, except . . .

Esa drew his six-gun and shot him in the head. Wilson fell from the saddle and landed with a dull thump on a prickly pear cactus.

'What the hell did you do that for?' Smith blurted out, shock on his face at the callous way in which Wilson had been dispatched.

'He was dyin',' Esa told him bluntly.

'But there was still no reason to kill him like that.'

'He was gutshot. Did you want him to go out of this world screamin' in pain, hollerin' for his mama?'

Smith knew Esa was right and remained silent.

'I didn't think so. Now come on. Let's go.'

7

'What the hell happened out there?' Perkins fumed. 'I send you out with a dozen men and you come back with almost half your number gone. Your orders were simply to stir up trouble, not get all your men killed.'

'They jumped us,' Esa tried to explain.

'Sir!'

'Sir.'

Esa went on to explain what happened at the Yavapai camp while Perkins listened in silence to the report.

'Is your wounded man going to make it?'

'Yeah,' Esa nodded. 'He'll be fine.'

Perkins paced to the window and stared out at the parade ground that glowed orange under the sinking sun. It was usually a magnificent time of the day, when the desert was transformed into something magical. He turned back to Esa and said, 'OK. With the bodies you left out there, it won't be long before we start to see the results. And when we do, we'll make contact with the Yavapai and offer them an alliance.'

That was the part of the plan that worried Esa. Rile up the Apaches to get them on side, and they'd just as likely slit your throat for being a white man.

'I hope you're right, sir,' Esa said. 'If you ain't, then we're all dead.'

'Then we'll all be beyond caring, won't we?'

There was a knock at the door and a private entered, a worried expression on his face.

'What is it, Spence?' Perkins snapped, annoyed at the interruption.

'I'm sorry, Major, but Captain Simeon doesn't seem to be anywhere on the post.'

Perkins frowned. 'Did you look everywhere?'

'Yes, sir.'

Perkins looked at Esa. 'Have you seen him since you've been back?'

'No. The last I heard, he was out lookin' for the escapees.'

'Are the others back?'

Spence nodded.

'Then where the hell is Simeon?'

Both men stared blankly at him.

'Damn it! Find out where he is.'

Perkins watched them leave and returned to his seat. He tried to work out what Simeon might be up to and where he'd gone. Each scenario he came up left him with a nagging feeling that once he found out, he wasn't going to like it.

* * *

'I asked you a question, Sloan. Now damn well answer it,' Esa snarled.

There was no love lost between the two men, and Sloan looked at him defiantly. 'I don't know,' he said. 'We lost contact with him. He told us to come on back while he checked out something he'd seen.'

'You're lyin'.'

Sloan shrugged. 'Maybe. But there ain't no way for you to prove it, is there?'

The was a drawn-out silence as Esa's icy stare lingered on him. A horse snorted in its stall further along the stables, while another shifted about noisily. The air was filled with the smell of straw and horse shit.

'I ought to beat the truth outa you here and now, you lyin' son of a bitch,' Esa growled, taking a step toward Sloane.

The dry triple-click of a gun hammer going back made Esa halt. Then he felt the gun barrel pressed hard to the back of his head.

'If you take one more step, Esa, I'll blow your damned brains all over the stables,' Sergeant Larry Granville whispered harshly so no one could overhear.

Esa showed no fear at the threat and said, 'Stay out of this, Granville. It ain't got nothin' to do with you.'

'He's my man, Esa. Leave him be. Get gone, Sloan.'

Esa turned slowly and faced the square-jawed Granville after Sloan had disappeared. Even though he was almost six feet tall, Granville had a further four inches on him.

'All I wanted to know was where Simeon was.'

'He told you. Now get.'

As Esa started to leave, Granville called after him. 'I know what you and Perkins are tryin' to do, Esa. Shelby told me. You're both mad, tryin' to use Apaches to help your cause. All you two stupid bastards will do is get the men killed. The cause is dead. Even the general knows it.'

Esa turned and said, 'This ain't over.'

'Yeah, it is,' Granville corrected him. 'Be gone.'

The big sergeant took one last look around the stables to see if there was anybody else there. Satisfied that he was alone, he turned and walked out the double doors that led onto the parade ground.

The air outside was chill against his skin and the sky was clear, so the moon and stars stood out brightly. Granville made to walk on when there was movement behind him. He whirled about to face Esa.

'What the hell . . . ?'

Granville got no further before his opposite number raised his six-gun and shot him in the face. The effect of the .44 caliber slug on human flesh and bone was devastating. It destroyed everything in its path until the back of Granville's head exploded violently outwards.

The body collapsed at Esa's feet with a dull thud. He looked down with disdain at the corpse and then hawked. He rolled the globule around in his mouth then spat on the dead man's ruined face.

He sniffed and said, 'Damned traitor.'

* * *

Somewhere in the moonlit darkness off to the east, a coyote yipped and finished with a drawn-out high-pitched howl. It was instantly answered by two more, one to the southeast and another to the northwest.

Savage poked at the small fire with a stick and said, 'I see you got some friends out there hangin' around.'

'They ain't coyotes,' Lucifer pointed out.

'I know. You want to hope they don't get you. They'll kill you nice and slow. Probably take a week. Peel the skin right off you.'

'What about you?'

'Hell, they'll probably kill me just for associatin' with you. I know I would.'

Lucifer's face grew hard and he said, 'I'll go and check the horses.'

'No,' said Savage with a shake of his head. 'I will.'

'Don't you trust me?' Lucifer sneered.

'I'd trust a coiled rattler before I'd trust you, Lucifer. Even them Apaches out there are more trustworthy than you.'

Lucifer's voice took on a hard edge. 'When this is done, you and me are gonna have a reckonin'.'

Savage ignored the remark and walked beyond the firelight to check on the horses. The coyotes started up again and the sorrel shifted nervously.

'Easy, horse,' he soothed. 'They won't be comin' tonight.'

The animal snorted as though it understood the calming words. Savage stood there beside the animal for a time staring out across the desert. He watched as inanimate figures like the giant saguaros seemingly took on life.

The Apaches called back and forth to one another, and Savage figured there were now at least five of them out there in the dark. He decided then that they would ride on before the sun came up, maybe even a couple of hours before dawn.

It would take at least another day and a half to reach the fort. Add another day turnaround before the cavalry headed back into the mountains.

Savage walked back into the firelight and saw that Lucifer had laid down beside the fire, back to him, trying to keep warm. He shrugged his shoulders and said sarcastically, 'I'll take first watch, shall I?'

Lucifer remained silent.

'Nope, I insist. Don't go gettin' up on my account.'

Nothing.

Savage frowned. He moved closer to the still form and noticed the dark stain on the sand beneath him. Hesitantly, he reached down and gripped Lucifer's shoulder and rolled him onto his back.

The man was dead. His throat had been slashed right across and gaped wide like some sort of macabre smile.

'Well now,' Savage said as he straightened and dropped his hand to the butt of the Remington, 'it looks like Lucifer has gone to hell.'

★   ★   ★

Everywhere he looked, the morning sky was filled with signal-smoke. North, east, west, and south. There was no escaping the fact that he was surrounded. Savage had left the campsite well before dawn. He'd left both Lucifer and his horse behind. The dead man's weapons, however, he'd kept. The Navy Colt he placed in his saddlebags, and the rifle was rolled up in his bedroll.

'Somethin's sure got them riled up, horse,' Savage said out loud to the sorrel. 'Surely it ain't because of Lucifer. All this smoke ain't from the Chiricahua. There's somethin' else goin' on. Somethin' big.'

The horse shifted uneasily beneath him and waited patiently as Savage took off his hat and wiped the sweat from his brow. He'd stopped to assess his options and studied the surrounding country. There was a faint dust haze in every direction except to the south of his position on the low ridge. It wasn't the way he wanted to go, but seemed to be the only avenue open to him and was more than likely the way the Apaches wanted him to go.

Savage reached down and took the Yellow Boy from the saddle scabbard. He checked the action and sat it with its butt resting on his right thigh. He eased the horse forward and said, 'Looks like things are about to get a whole lot more interestin'.'

Savage chose to go west. Not because he wanted to, but because that was the most direct route to Fort Craig. He rode between two giant saguaros and followed the faint trail down the slope before he cut off it and dropped down into a dry wash.

He followed its winding path for two miles until the sound of horse hooves rumbling across the desert reached his ears. He hauled back on the reins and brought the sorrel to a halt. Then he spotted them. Their track would bring them within fifty yards of his position.

Savage urged the sorrel forward until it was hidden behind a clump of brush at the edge of the wash. He dismounted and stood near the sorrel's head and rubbed its muzzle to keep it quiet while the strange horses passed.

The drumming grew louder and he could see them clearly when he peered around the edge of the clump. Thirty of them. Their long black hair bounced against brown shoulders covered in dust kicked up by their horses as they cantered along.

The sorrel surged against Savage's grip and he fought to keep it from breaking loose. As the drumming grew quieter, it settled again, and all that was left of the Apaches passing was the billowing cloud of dust.

Savage climbed back into the saddle. 'Come on, horse. It's time we got the hell outa here.'

★　★　★

Ben Simeon saw the same smoke Savage had seen that morning and cursed Perkins and his lunatic scheme.

This entire part of Arizona Territory was about to have the lid blown off, and Perkins was too wrapped up in his own world and blinded by his cause to see how dangerous the situation could become. He'd pushed his horse for most of the night, but the animal was tired. He knew that if he didn't locate Savage soon, he would be forced to stop for a long period for his mount to rest.

Without warning, the ground in front of him heaved and exploded upwards as a figure came clear of the depression it had been hiding in. The renegade Rios had managed to circle around to get in front of Simeon and had buried himself just to the left of the trail to wait for his quarry. He brought up a battered Spencer repeating rifle and aimed it at Simeon.

The hammer on the rifle fell and the sound of the gunshot rocked the surrounding desert. Just before the bullet knocked the captain from his horse, he could see the look of triumph on the renegade's face.

The impact of the heavy caliber slug felt like a hammer blow to his chest and as he fell, Simeon's body became numb from the shock of it. He hit the ground hard, his face planted firmly into the coarse sand. Unable to move, he could hear Rios approach. The sound of his footsteps was followed by a shadow that fell across him.

Rios prodded at the open wound in Simeon's back where the bullet from the Spencer had exited. The captain stiffened and screamed as pain shot through his body.

'Good,' Rios hissed in a low voice. 'You are still alive. But you will soon be dead.'

The renegade bent down and grabbed the prone Simeon roughly by the shoulder and rolled him onto his back. The killer's eyes flew wide when he found himself staring down the barrel of Simeon's six-gun.

'Eat this, you son of a bitch,' Simeon

said, his cold smile exposing blood-stained teeth.

The gun crashed loudly and spewed a mix of flame and blue-gray smoke from its barrel. The slug smashed into Rios's face, blowing brain matter and bone fragments from the back of his head. The lifeless body fell to the ground with a dull thud and Simeon snarled wetly, 'Got you, you bastard. Damn well . . . '

He coughed and a rattle emanated from deep within his chest. 'I guess you got me too. And good.'

Simeon tried to sit up, but the pain from his wound wracked his body and stopped his attempt. He tried again, gritting his teeth and clenching his jaw to counteract the blinding pain. He let himself fall back and lay panting from the exertion.

He decided to take a minute before having another go. There was a strange sensation from deep in his chest as it started to fill with blood. He looked up at the cloudless sky, the pale blue seemingly endless. While he stared out at it, every breath grew shallower until eventually he stopped breathing altogether.

Twenty minutes later, as if on cue, a vulture began to turn lazy circles overhead. It was soon joined by several more. Before long, the first of the carrion eaters landed. It waddled cautiously over to the closest corpse, looked it over to make sure it was dead, and sank its sharp-pointed beak into Simeon's right eye.

8

Savage knew that trouble had found him the moment a small covey of quail broke from a clump of acacia. Their wings beat furiously at the air in an effort to escape what had startled them. He drew back on the horse's reins and made sure to keep his hands away from his weapons.

Apart from his horse's breath, the desert was silent. Nothing moved. He waited for a full minute before a mounted Apache appeared to his right, quickly followed by two more. Then four came up on his left. As around another forty came thundering up from behind, a single Apache moved to stand in front of Savage and block the sorrel's path.

He wore a red bandanna around his head, which kept long black hair from his face. His dark eyes were deeply set in his bronzed face, and his clothing consisted of leggings and a stained shirt.

When he stepped forward, he carried himself with great pride. He stared up at Savage and said in fluent Spanish, 'I see you, Jeff Savage. It has been a while.'

Savage nodded in agreement. 'Hello, Cochise.'

★　★　★

'I say we kill him now,' he heard a thin sinewy brave say loudly. 'Let us feed him to the ants and the buzzards while the sun burns out his eyes.'

Cochise stared unwaveringly at Savage, who sat on the sand with his hands tied behind his back. The last time Savage and the fearsome Apache chief had met, it had been under much better circumstances. In fact, the chief had only been a brave when they'd first encountered each other.

It had been back in the days when Savage worked as a freighter shipping goods along the overland stage route. The freight outfit had been attacked by a band of twenty Chiricahua out looking for horses and guns. They'd hit late in the afternoon, coming out of the sunset, using the glare in their favor. After a brief but fierce battle, they'd pulled back but left two dead freighters and five dead braves. And a wounded Cochise.

The others had wanted to shoot the wounded brave on sight but Savage would have no part in it. He stood defiantly against his fellow teamsters, and in the end he won out and Cochise was released. Savage was reasonably sure it was the reason he was still alive so far and hadn't been skinned alive. His only hope was that his luck would hold out long enough to try and convince Cochise to let him go.

Savage looked about at the other paint-daubed faces that stared coldly in his direction. All because of that bastard Lucifer.

Cochise and the others had been arguing for hours, and it was now late in the afternoon. Savage was cramped, and his mouth felt as dry as the desert they were in.

Suddenly there was an outburst, and the sinewy brave threw his arms up in the air and stormed off. Cochise rose and walked over to where Savage sat with his back against an uncomfortable rock.

'What's the verdict?' he asked.

Cochise shrugged. 'Maybe you die, maybe you live. It is still not decided. Most of my warriors want you dead. The others will leave that decision for me to make.'

'Your friend didn't look too happy with that idea.'

'That is because his brother was killed by a white man who takes hair some days ago,' Cochise explained. 'He wants all white eyes to pay for it. You ride the land of the Yavapai at a bad time, Jeff Savage.'

'Why are your people in the land of the Yavapai?'

'The man who killed Chaco's brother also killed others for their hair. We ride to avenge them. And to kill him.'

'So it was your people who attacked the Concho Springs stage station?'

Cochise nodded.

'But why? They did nothin' to you or your people. It was just plain murder.'

'And what do you call the killing of our people?' Cochise spat angrily.

He was right. But their retribution against the innocent wasn't. 'And you let that feller go with a message for the fort?'

Cochise nodded again.

'What is goin' on with the Yavapai?' Savage asked.

'Bluecoat soldiers rode against a small group of Yavapai yesterday. They killed not only men but women and children.'

Savage thought about what the chief had just told him. The colonel had said nothing about sending troops into the mountains. He was concentrating his patrols elsewhere.

'Are they certain that it was blue-coats?' Savage asked.

Cochise nodded grimly. 'They left some of their dead behind.'

Savage shook his head. 'I don't understand it. I left the fort the day after you and your braves hit Concho Springs, and the commander there was gonna concentrate his forces lookin' for the Chiricahua. He said he was gonna stay away from here and I guess step up patrols to protect the trails and such while he was at it.'

'Why are you here?' Cochise asked the obvious question.

'Lookin' for a half-breed feller called Rios. The army wanted me to hunt him and his renegades down.'

Savage went on to elaborate his past days and what he was doing when the Chiricahuas had picked him up.

'It is a shame you did not kill that one,' Cochise said. 'He is bad.'

'Yeah, I've seen his work. On the

96

other hand, though, the feller you're lookin' for is dead.'

Cochise turned his head to look into the eyes of his captive. 'What do you mean, dead?'

'Last night,' Savage explained. 'I was checkin' the horses and when I went back, I found him dead with his throat cut. I was wonderin' if it was your braves, but I'm guessin' it was Yavapai.'

Cochise shook his head.

'So I guess you fellers can all go home now,' Savage proposed. 'Now that the feller you want is dead and all.'

Again Cochise shook his head. 'The Yavapai have asked us for our help to fight the blue-coats. We will ride to join them.'

'But why? It couldn't have been the soldiers from Fort Craig who did it. I told you they aren't even up here.'

'Then who else?' Cochise snapped.

Savage's shoulders slumped. 'I don't know.'

Cochise stood up to leave.

'What now?'

'I go to talk to the others and see if they will let you live,' Cochise explained.

'Thank you.'

'I will do my best,' Cochise said. 'I have not forgotten that I owe you my life.'

'I was kinda hopin' you would remember.'

'It doesn't mean that you will live. I may be chief, but I am also one man, and at this time we are at war with the white-eyes.'

★　★　★

While Cochise was gone, Savage sat and thought about what the chief had told him. There was no way that the colonel had men here in the mountains. It raised all sorts of questions. Like who could it have been, and why? Who would gain by doing it? It wasn't scalp hunters.

If they had been dressed in Reb uniforms, then it could have been them, but they hadn't been. Whoever it was would supposedly be long gone by now, otherwise they'd have a whole army of Apaches coming down on them. A whole army . . .

'Son of a bitch,' Savage said out loud. 'No. He wouldn't be so stupid.'

His mind went back to the dinner with Shelby and how the general had told him of the crazy Perkins. The man needed a big army or a whole lot of fanatical fighters like himself. And if he could rile up the Apaches and get them onside, then he would have his worked-up force of fighters. They would face the common enemy together. And he guessed that their first target would be Fort Craig.

★ ★ ★

It was dark when Cochise returned, though not with the news that Savage had hoped for. Instead, he said to him, 'Tomorrow you shall fight for your freedom. It will be a fight to the death with knives.'

'Who?'

'Chaco.'

'Hell,' sighed Savage.

'It is the best I could do.'

Savage nodded. 'Thanks. I think.'

Cochise just grunted.

'I been thinkin' about what you said. You know, about those blue-coats that killed the Yavapai.'

'Yes?'

'I don't think they were blue-coats,' Savage said. 'It was Rebs dressed that way.'

'Why would they do that?' Cochise asked.

Savage explained the thinking behind it, then asked, 'What are the Yavapai plannin'?'

Cochise just stared at him, the orange light of the flickering fire dancing shadows across his face. 'I do not know.'

'If I win this fight tomorrow, will you take your people home?'

'No.'

'You have to trust me, Cochise. I'm right about this. If you and your braves continue to wage war in this territory, then a lot of you will die for something that is beyond your control. This whole thing has been manipulated by a damned maniac.'

'And what of the Yavapai?' Cochise asked.

'I will do my best to stop this. Whatever it is. The Rebs have a great chief, like you, and if anyone can help me stop it, it's him.'

'What about the one you say is responsible?'

'If it's true, then I'll kill him myself,' Savage told him.

'But first you have to face Chaco.'

'Yeah, Chaco.'

* * *

'Tomorrow, Sergeant,' Perkins said with finality, 'we'll take a column of men out and strike a bargain with the Yavapai.'

101

'And if they don't listen?'

'They'll listen,' Perkins said confidently. 'I want you to put fifty rifles from our store into a wagon and we'll take it with us.'

'Are you sure that's — '

'Just damn well do it,' Perkins snapped.

'Yes, sir.'

'Hand pick the men,' Perkins told him. 'I want soldiers who have undying loyalty to the cause.'

Esa nodded. 'Who are you gonna leave in charge of the fort?'

'Is Simeon back yet?'

'No.'

'Then I'll have to leave you in charge.'

'I think I should be along with you, sir.'

'You are the only one I trust to do the job,' Perkins told him.

'And if Simeon shows, lock him away with his commanding officer for being off post. At least that way I shall be rid of him.'

* * *

The sun was a flaming ball of orange in the cloudless sky the next morning when Savage and Chaco finally squared off against one another. The sinewy Apache was shirtless, and each move he made caused his muscles to ripple. The desert heat had already brought about a thin sheen to his body.

The adversaries were encircled by nearly all of the Chiricahua raiding party, bodies creating an almost impenetrable barrier. Cochise moved forward and offered Savage his own knife.

'Know this,' he said to Savage. 'If you die, I shall do my best to see that the Yavapai are not fooled by the white-eye you talked about.'

'That's right kind of you,' Savage said sarcastically as he removed his shirt. 'I'll die a lot happier knowin' that.'

Cochise stepped back and left the two combatants to their arena. Chaco faced Savage with a look of utter disdain. He held a wicked-looking knife in his right hand. He spat on the ground in disgust and moved in. Savage knew that should the fight continue for a prolonged period of time, he was a dead man. Chaco would have the stamina to outlast him.

Chaco wasted no time and lunged in, his blade slicing thin air as Savage sucked in his belly and jumped back. The warrior moved again, this time taking a back-handed swipe at Savage, who narrowly managed to avoid it. Savage launched his own brief attack. His knife hand streaked out and a hiss escaped Chaco's lips as the knife scored the flesh of the warrior's right arm, bringing forth a thin trickle of bright red blood.

The warrior didn't bother to check the wound but moved in for another attack. The sun flickered off the Indian's blade as he aimed for Savage's belly, intent on disemboweling him.

Savage blocked the scything blow with his own knife and the blades rang out when they met. Chaco grunted in surprise at Savage's swiftness.

Both men backed away and circled to the right before Chaco moved to engage again. He feinted left, then cut back right and nicked the skin of Savage's midsection. Savage jumped back at the burning sensation and knew instantly he'd been cut. But he dared not look down. To take his eyes from Chaco meant the Apache would take advantage and be on him in a heartbeat. He could feel the blood trickle down his front; and as sweat met the open wound, his flesh stung sharply. Chaco smiled coldly, then lunged forward and didn't stop.

Savage caught his knife-arm just below the wrist, and Chaco did the same. The Apache was powerful, and Savage used it to his advantage. Instead of trying to stop the charge of Chaco, he fell backward, bringing Chaco with him. When Savage hit the ground, he brought his legs up and used them as a lever. The Apache's momentum and the thrust of Savage's legs helped Chaco to sail forward over Savage's head. He hit the compact desert sand with a loud *whoof*, rolled and came cat-like to his feet. Savage was only halfway to his when Chaco launched another attack.

Chaco hit him hard and knocked him onto his back, the snarling Apache coming down on top of him. The knife slid from Savage's grip from the impact, but he needed both hands free to grasp Chaco's wrists in an attempt to stop the razor-sharp blade being driven down into his throat.

Their faces were only inches apart as they both struggled. Chaco grimaced as he tried to force the blade down even further. Savage felt the point prick the skin just below his chin. Fear and adrenaline surged through his body at the thought he was about to die. He heaved with all his strength and threw Chaco to the side.

Once more, the Apache regained his feet quickly while Savage got to his and scooped up his knife. Chaco came at him again. The knife flicked forward and back and before Savage knew it, he was bleeding from a second cut to his chest.

Blood flowed freely now as the new one was deeper than the first. The Apache came at him again, and Savage lashed out with his boot. He connected with Chaco's knife arm but didn't dislodge the knife.

Savage waited for Chaco to make a mistake. The Apache, on the other hand, was growing impatient and frustrated. He'd expected Savage to show more fear, thus making him easier to kill. But he was wrong, and his frustration was making him sloppy. He lunged in carelessly, and Savage opened a good sized cut on his left side.

An audible murmur rippled through the gathered onlookers as Chaco stepped back to take stock. But Savage followed him; and with a thrust and flick of the knife, he opened up another cut to the Apache's muscular right arm, his knife arm. Blood flowed freely from both wounds but the one in the right arm bled more, running down the arm and across the knife handle, making it slick.

That was when Savage noticed a look of fear in Chaco's eyes. Fear that the white-eyes might actually win, ensuring his own death; or worse, make him lose honor in the eyes of his tribe.

The warrior's face became like granite. That would not happen. When he came forward with blinding speed, he found Savage up to the task. There was a flurry of arms and blades; and when it stopped, Savage moved past Chaco and stood with his back to the warrior, facing some of the gathered Apaches.

Chaco was doing the same, except there was a confused expression on his face. One of absolute puzzlement. A slow rivulet of bright red blood issued from a thin line across his throat. He moved his head, and the trickle became a torrent of red flowing over his muscular chest as the cut opened right across the Apache's throat.

Chaco sank to his knees, eyes still wide. He knelt there for what seemed like an age before he fell face first into the sand.

Savage knew he'd killed Chaco even without turning to see. In the flurry of movement, he'd somehow found an opening and slashed the blade across the exposed throat. His shoulders slumped with relief, but he remained still.

A Chiricahua brave stepped forward with his rifle raised ready to kill Savage, when a loud command from Cochise stopped him. The warrior spat on the ground at Savage's feet and snarled words that he couldn't understand before whirling and pushing his way through the crush.

'I see you still live, Jeff Savage,' Cochise said from beside him. 'None have faced the blade of Chaco before and escaped.'

'Maybe that's why I was able to beat him,' Savage surmised. 'Maybe he was overconfident and got careless. Or maybe I just like livin' and weren't ready to die yet.'

'Maybe.'

Savage checked his wounds.

'You will need them seen to before you go,' Cochise pointed out.

'So I'm able to leave?' Savage asked.

The Apache chief nodded. 'No one will try to stop you.'

'Are you takin' your warriors back to their lands?'

'Yes,' Cochise answered. 'We will go back now. What about you? Are you going to try to stop the white-eye who wishes war?'

'Yes, before it's too late.'

Savage went to hand the knife to Cochise.

'Keep it,' he told him. 'You may have more need of it than I.'

Twenty minutes later, Savage was ready to leave. His wounds had been cleaned and dressed and his weapons and horse returned to him. But if he thought he was going to get away unscathed, then he thought wrong. He was tightening his cinch when Cochise came up behind him and said, 'You will take something else with you when you leave.'

Savage turned and immediately froze. Standing in front of him was a woman with long dark disheveled hair and red-rimmed green eyes. He stared at her for a long drawn-out moment of silence, then said, 'Ahh hell no.'

'I still ain't forgot you hit me and killed my man, you son of a bitch,' Gloria Tate snarled.

Savage shook his head and looked at Cochise. 'I'm gonna need a horse for her.'

'I will see that you get one.'

'You know she tried to kill me?'

'Me too,' Cochise said. 'Twice.'

The Apache chief walked away to get another horse for the woman.

'I heard you died along with the rest of them,' Savage told her.

Gloria lifted her chin defiantly and said, 'Not hardly.'

'OK, listen up. If you want to come

with me, then you'll do as I say. If not, I'll just leave your pretty little ass here and Cochise can deal with you.'

Gloria's eyes flared, but she allowed herself to calm before she spoke. 'You wouldn't dare,' she said with a hint of indignation in her voice.

He glared at her. 'Just damn well try me.'

Gloria set her jaw firm but remained silent. Then her expression softened. 'You think I'm pretty?'

Savage gave her an exasperated look. 'Oh, shut up.'

A couple of minutes later, Cochise returned with a pinto. 'The horse is a little spirited, but it will do.'

'That'll make two of them.'

'Good luck, Jeff Savage,' Cochise said. 'I hope you succeed in stopping the white-eye.'

9

Through the small window of his cell, Shelby watched as the wagon was loaded with rifles. All the while he cursed the man who'd taken over his command and was about to get most of them killed.

'Dumb stupid son of a bitch,' he swore out loud.

Then he watched as fifty men rode out in two columns led by the same stupid son of a bitch.

'Private Rutledge,' he called out to the man on guard.

'What do you want?'

'I want you to get Sergeant Brown for me.'

'Can't do that, sir.'

'Damn it, man. Do you know what they took out of here in that wagon?'

'Ain't my job to ask.'

'They took rifles. Rifles! And do you

know where they're taking them?'

This time Rutledge didn't speak.

'They're taking them to the Apaches,' Shelby told him. 'Perkins thinks he can get them to side with him against the Union. He thinks he can make them a part of his new army.'

Rutledge still remained silent.

'Now you and I both know that the only thing the Apaches are going to do with them rifles is kill them all. So they have to be stopped. Now get Brown for me.'

Rutledge hesitated once more, but decided that what Shelby had said made sense and went to fetch Esa Brown.

It was ten minutes before he returned with Esa, who entered the cell and glared at Shelby. 'What do you want?' he asked in a disrespectful tone.

'I want you to let me out of here before it's too late,' Shelby answered.

Esa snorted. 'That ain't gonna happen.'

'Damn it, Esa,' Shelby barked, 'that

son of a bitch is going to get all of them killed. Perkins doesn't have a clue what'll happen once the Apaches get the rifles.'

Esa stood firm, his loyalty to his commanding officer and the cause overriding any doubts that he had. 'Major Perkins knows what he's doin',' he stated firmly. 'Now shut your yowlin'. You ain't gettin' out.'

He turned, walked out, and left Shelby to fume on his own.

'This will be on your head, Esa!' he raged. 'Yours and that stupid bastard you blindly follow.'

★   ★   ★

It was the middle of the afternoon when Savage drew rein and unsheathed the Yellow Boy, jacking a round into its breech. The sun burned hot against their exposed skin as it hung in the cloudless sky.

'What's wrong?' Gloria Tate asked, an edge to her voice.

'Somethin's dead,' Savage told her in a soft tone. 'Up ahead. I can make out the buzzards.'

Gloria strained to see across the desert. At first she could make out nothing, but after a couple of moments she could just see the waddling black shapes as they gorged themselves on whatever it was.

'Stay close,' Savage ordered. 'And if I tell you to ride, you ride like hell and don't look back. If you continue east for a day or so, you should make Shelby's valley.'

'Can't we go around?' Gloria asked, her voice filled with hope.

'Just keep quiet and follow me,' Savage said as he eased the sorrel forward.

As he rode, his eyes never stopped scanning the surrounding terrain. The smoke had stopped earlier, but it didn't mean that the Yavapai had gone. At one point, they had been forced to take refuge in a wash as a dust cloud had loomed to the south. Fortunately it had faded then vanished.

The scent of rotting flesh reached them as the breeze sprang up and carried the nauseating aroma across the final thirty yards to them. As the black carrion eaters went about their grisly task, Savage immediately thought of Amy. Pain stabbed at his heart, the thought of her still raw.

It wasn't until they were almost on top of them that Savage realized that there were two corpses providing a feast for the birds. 'Stay back,' he ordered Gloria. 'You don't need to see this.'

'Oh my Lord,' Gloria groaned as she saw the remains. Between the sight and the smell, it was too overwhelming, and she leaned sideways in the saddle and heaved.

Before dismounting, Savage glanced about. Seeing nothing out of the ordinary, he climbed down and looked the two corpses over. The gorged birds shuffled away, unwilling or unable to fly.

The first one was an Indian; that

much he could make out. Who it was, was anybody's guess. Savage moved on to the next one, and even though most of the face was gone, he still knew that it was Ben Simeon.

'What on earth were you doin' out here?' Savage said aloud.

With an air of urgency, Savage looked around some more and found that he'd not been the only one to come across the two dead men. There were the tracks of at least four sets of moccasins, which begged the question of why they hadn't scalped Simeon and taken care of their own dead. Unless the dead Apache wasn't one of theirs. Then that would make him the renegade Rios.

One problem solved, Savage thought.

'Can we go now?' Gloria Tate called from behind him.

Savage turned to see her wiping her mouth, trying to rid herself of the taste and smell of her stomach contents. He ignored her while he cast a sorrowful glance at Simeon's corpse.

'Sorry I can't do much for you,' Savage mumbled. 'But I reckon you would understand.'

Savage walked back to the sorrel. Without saying a word, he mounted and pointed it in the direction of Shelby's valley, still nagged by the unanswered question. What was Simeon doing out here?

★   ★   ★

Major Christopher Perkins halted his column ten miles from Fort Jackson by a small seasonal stream that held barely enough water for the men, let alone the horses. He posted pickets, then set about waiting for the Yavapai to find him. It was almost dusk, and the last orange fingers of sunlight reached out across the darkening sky. He placed the wagon full of rifles at the center of his camp.

Perkins recalled the Apache war smoke that had dotted the sky for most of the day and smiled to himself. His plan was starting to come together. All he needed now was a treaty with the Indians, and his force would be strong enough to put in motion his dream of making Texas, and the South, great again.

It wasn't much after dark when the Yavapai announced their presence. The air had cooled quickly once the sun had gone and small pinpricks of starlight started to fill the broad, cloudless sky. Out in the desert, the first yip of a coyote could be heard. It was followed by another off to the south. Soon the night was filled with them as they called back and forth to each other. The horses stirred nervously at their lines, stamping and snorting.

'What are we gonna do, sir?' a trooper named Crow asked Perkins. 'They're all around us.'

'We'll wait for morning, then see,' was all Perkins said. 'Tell Waters to have the men stand to just in case.'

★   ★   ★

Savage made a dry camp amongst some rocks and brush that evening a hundred or so yards off the trail. They made do with the water they had and built a small fire to keep warm.

'Why are you going back to warn them soldier boys when we should be getting the hell outa these mountains?' Gloria asked him from across the flickering orange flames.

'Because I told Shelby I'd help him,' Savage explained. 'And I told Cochise I was gonna try and stop a damned Indian war.'

'He's only a heathen,' she spat. 'Why keep your word to him?'

'Because when I give my word, I keep it,' Savage said. 'Unlike some.'

Her gaze grew hard. 'So do I.'

He knew what she was getting at. Her hate still ran deep even though she refused to show it, for the moment at least.

'How did a pretty Southern girl like you get mixed up with a no-good sonuver like Ned Tate?' Savage asked her.

'What's it to you?' she snapped.

'I'm curious is all. I mean, under all that dirt and grime you are a mighty handsome woman. You could have almost any man you set your sights on and yet you settle for a killer like Tate.'

'He wasn't always like that,' Gloria said. 'He was a good man once, before the war. We had everything until you damn Yankees decided to ruin it. After that, things were never the same. We lost everything. Our home, money, lifestyle, even our friends. So Ned turned to the only thing he had left. Gambling.'

'That turned out well for you,' Savage said coldly.

'We did what we had to do to survive,' Gloria snarled.

'Includin' murder.'

Gloria remained silent.

'You'd best turn in. We got a hard day ahead tomorrow.'

Gloria stared at him for a brief moment, and he wondered if she were about to say something. Instead, she turned her back on him and found a place to sleep.

* * *

Savage woke up the instant he felt something was wrong. It was like an inbuilt sixth sense that dragged him from the depths of darkness. His eyes snapped open wide and he saw the shadow that loomed ominously above him. He caught the glint of silvery moonlight upon a knife blade as it was lifted high, ready to plunge down in a killing blow.

Without a second thought, Savage rolled away from the descending knife, and it drove harmlessly into the sandy soil where he'd been lying. He lashed out with his boot and caught his attacker in the leg, making them buckle. A scream of pain and frustration told him who his assailant was.

Savage came up off the ground and moved in close to Gloria. She raised herself to one knee and brought the knife up, ready to slice across his stomach in a disemboweling stroke. He dodged it easily and with a chopping motion brought the heel of his hand down onto her wrist. The knife was dislodged and it fell harmlessly to the ground.

Another scream of frustration filled the surrounding desert as Gloria came up with hands curled into claws and tried to viciously rake his face. Savage took her by the wrists and held them in a firm grip. She snarled wildly at him, trying to bite exposed flesh.

'You murdering bastard!' she screamed. 'I'll kill you! I'll kill you! Be damned if I don't!'

Her struggles grew in intensity as she tried to break Savage's hold. With the speed of a striking rattler, Savage's right hand released its grip and shot forward, slapping Gloria across her cheek. Not too hard like the first time at Concho Springs, but hard enough to make her stop.

As her struggles ceased, he could

make out her blazing eyes in the dying firelight, filled with rage at the man who'd killed her husband.

And then for some strange reason, he kissed her. A hard, brutal kiss that mashed her lips against her teeth.

Gloria struggled to break away from him. Not like before, however. This time her efforts were feeble, and it wasn't long before she responded to his embrace and returned the kiss.

Then he pushed her away; a forceful shove that made her stagger and fall to her backside. He bent down and picked up the knife she'd tried to use. Gloria looked up at him, a confused expression on her face.

'What the hell was that?' Gloria snapped.

Savage stared at her in silence before he answered in a cold voice, 'I wanted to see if you really loved your husband or would settle for anyone who showed an interest. I guess I found out.'

'You son of a bitch,' she snarled. 'You low-down bastard.'

'Just you remember it,' he said, turning away.

But there was something about this woman, something that stirred him deep inside, and he didn't like it. It was an attraction of sorts brought on by her beauty and the fire from within. Not like Amy. She had been different, and he guessed that was why he felt a pang of guilt in his chest.

He turned back to face Gloria. 'Tell me one thing,' he said.

'What?'

'The feller they said you killed. The one that won your husband's money. Did you really kill him?'

Gloria stared at him and thought about telling him to go to hell, but for some strange reason decided against it. She shook her head. 'No. No, that wasn't me. Ned did that. I didn't even know about it until afterward.'

'Did you ever kill anyone for him?'

Again she shook her head. 'No.'

'Then why try to kill me?'

'After all,' Gloria told him, 'Ned was

still my husband, and I loved him.'

Savage nodded his understanding. 'Get some sleep.'

He settled back down under his blanket and closed his eyes, mind still whirling from the previous events. Then came the soft footfall from beside him.

'Are you gonna try and kill me again?' he asked. 'You got another knife I don't know about?'

'I'm cold,' Gloria said.

Savage opened his eyes and looked up at her. He felt the stirring again and knew this time it wasn't going to go away. He didn't say anything, just drew back the blanket for her. It was a long while before they both found sleep.

⋆　⋆　⋆

The sun had just started to claw its way into a cloudless sky when Savage broke camp the following morning. He'd saddled the sorrel and was seeing to the pinto when Gloria approached.

'I tried to hire Lucifer to kill you, you

know,' she informed him. 'But he wouldn't do it.'

'Uh huh,' Savage grunted, not looking at her.

She studied him for a moment, then asked, 'What was her name?'

Savage turned. 'Who?'

'Your wife.'

'Amy.'

'What was she like?'

'Why?' Savage asked, trying to avoid the question.

'Is it true that you killed all them men?'

'Damn it,' Savage snapped, 'what is this?'

'I guess I'd like to know a little about the man I shared a bed with,' Gloria answered.

'Let's get one thing straight,' Savage said forcefully. 'Last night was a one-off. It ain't never gonna happen again. Got it?'

Gloria's mouth fell open and her eyes showed the hurt of his scathing words. Then the pain spread across her face, etched deep; and when she tried to speak, nothing came out. She took a faltering step towards Savage, then fell forward, revealing the arrow buried between her shoulder blades.

Savage's military training took over as he dragged his gaze from the dead woman. Used to making split decisions under pressure, he leaped to the sorrel's side and dragged the Yellow Boy Winchester from the scabbard. He whirled just as a painted Apache emerged whooping from some rocks, a wicked-looking knife in his right hand.

The rifle in Savage's grasp thundered and the slug that blasted from its barrel slammed into the warrior's bare middle with a loud thwack. The Apache grunted from the impact and went to his knees incapacitated, the knife dropped beside him.

The *pfzzt* sound of an arrow passing close to him drew Savage's attention to the brush that was directly behind where Gloria had been standing. An Apache with a bow was now visible, trying to nock another arrow to loose at his quarry.

The Yellow Boy roared again, and the Apache was punched back as the .44 Henry slug slammed violently into his chest. He fell into the brush, and the only thing left protruding were his feet as they beat a death tattoo on the dry ground.

Savage worked the rifle's lever, and another cartridge slammed home into the breech. There was movement to his left, and a third paint-daubed Apache appeared. This one, though, had a battered Spencer rifle and was bringing it up to fire. Without thinking, Savage rolled to his right and came up on one knee. The warrior had fired the Spencer and the slug dug into the sand to his left.

The rifle bucked, and the warrior howled with pain as the bullet hit him in the right shoulder, causing him to drop the Spencer. Immediately the wounded Apache pulled a knife from its sheath on his hip and started forward.

'Stop right there,' Savage ordered him in Spanish. 'You don't have to die today.'

The Indian ignored him and kept coming, a menacing snarl upon his face. Savage fired and a red blossom appeared on the Apache's chest, staining what used to be a light-colored shirt, causing him to drop like a stone.

Yet another Apache emerged from some rocks directly in front of him, causing Savage to wonder how many more there were. This one was armed with a bow, like the one who'd killed Gloria. He leveled the Winchester and fired four fast shots that plowed into the ground at the advancing warrior's feet.

The Apache turned and ran, not wanting to end up dead like his brothers. Savage watched him as he disappeared into the rocks and brush, and it wasn't long before the sound of retreating horse hooves could be heard.

He climbed to his feet, eyes scanning the surrounding landscape as he searched for any further danger. After a minute of doing so, no more Apaches appeared.

Savage walked over and stood beside the dead form of Gloria Tate, and when he looked down at her unmoving body he realized that he felt nothing. He was devoid of emotion towards her death and put it down to the murder of his wife and the events that had followed. Even though he'd spent the night with her, he still felt no sadness or regret.

He looked around once more and saw the puffs of white-gray smoke start to rise to the north. 'Sorry, Gloria,' he said grimly. 'The earth will have to claim you in its own way. Time to go.'

Savage turned and . . . 'Ahh hell. Bastard.'

The sorrel was dead with an arrow protruding from its chest. He'd been so caught up in staying alive, he hadn't noticed that the horse had been hit. At least the pinto was still alive.

Hurrying as fast as possible, Savage changed the saddle and everything else over to the paint. By the time he was ready, a dust cloud could be seen rising from the same direction that he'd seen the smoke.

'Just in time,' he muttered, and mounted. He heeled the pinto hard, and it lunged forward into a ground-eating gait.

10

'Sir, look!' a trooper called out to Perkins, who turned to stare in the direction the man had indicated. He raised his hand to fend off the glare of the sun; then he saw them. On a ridge some three hundred yards distant, sitting atop motionless horses amongst scattered saguaros, was a line of at least eighty Apaches.

'What do you want to do, sir?' Waters asked as he approached Perkins and stood at his side. He was a big man with dark hair and an undying passion for the Confederacy.

Without taking his eyes from the imposing line, Perkins said, 'Get that flag-of-truce I had you make up last night, and a rifle. Then come back here. We're goin' for a walk.'

Waters did as he was ordered and returned with both of the items required.

Perkins turned and looked for Crow, and found him staring up at the ridge. 'Crow,' he called, 'if anything happens to us, form up the men and fight your way back to Fort Jackson. Don't get penned up here.'

'Yes, sir.'

The two men walked out beyond the camp under the fluttering white rag that was supposed to ensure their safety. But how many times had Indians been slaughtered under a flag of truce?

Five riders started down the slope towards the two advancing men. The groups met around a hundred yards from the Confederate encampment.

'What is it you want, white-eye?' a middle-aged Apache on a wiry mustang asked abruptly in halting English.

Perkins's gaze drifted over all of the fearsome-looking Indians with their faces painted for war and wondered if he was doing the right thing. 'My name is Major Christopher Perkins and I have come to talk to the chief of the Yavapai-Apache.'

'Then you shall talk to me,' the Apache said. 'I am called Delshay. Make it quick before I have my warriors kill you all.'

'Well now, that would certainly be an inconvenience to both of us, wouldn't it? Especially with what I have in that wagon.'

There was a flicker of interest in Delshay's eyes. 'Speak,' he said with more than a hint of irritation.

'I have fifty Spencer rifles in that wagon,' Perkins explained. 'Just like this one.' He motioned to Waters to hand the rifle over.

Delshay took it in calloused hands and looked it over. If there was any emotion flowing through the Apache chief, he kept it well hidden. After a minute or so, he nodded his approval and handed it back. 'You say you have fifty of these?'

'I do.'

'What you want for them? Gold? Money?'

'I want your help.'

Delshay looked puzzled.

'You and I have a common enemy — the blue-coats. I want us to join forces to fight that enemy.'

The Apache chief looked skeptical. 'Why should I join forces with you when I can fight them myself?'

'I can supply your warriors with the rifles that they will need, and you can supply fighters that will help me with my cause. You and your people will be able to take your land back from the white-eyes, and I'll be able to rid Texas of the invaders.'

'All that for just fifty rifles?' Delshay snorted derisively.

Perkins shook his head. 'No. I can get you another hundred.'

There was a hint of interest in the Apache chief's eyes at the mention of the number of rifles. He thought in silence, then nodded. 'I talk to some of my people and then I tell you.' Without waiting for a reply, he whirled his horse about and rode back up the slope, followed by the other four Apaches.

Waters breathed out slowly and said, 'That went well. I think.'

'We're still alive, so that counts for something,' Perkins allowed.

★ ★ ★

They waited for half an hour before the same five Apaches came riding back down the slope and stopped in front of the two men.

'We have talked and decided that we will accept your terms,' Delshay told Perkins.

'That's good,' Perkins said with a smile.

'But we want rifles now,' the Apache chief told them. 'All rifles.'

Perkins stared at him warily. 'We only have the fifty with us.'

The Apache's gaze grew icy. 'We take them. You bring rest here in two days.'

From the look Delshay was giving him, Perkins knew there was no arguing with him. 'Deal,' he said, offering his hand.

Delshay curled his lip into a sneer and turned his horse away. Perkins and Waters watched them go.

'I don't like it,' Waters muttered.

'Neither do I,' Perkins acknowledged, as he showed doubt for the first time. 'But we've come too far now. Get the wagon and bring it out here and leave it.'

Fifteen minutes later, the troop was formed up and ready to move out. The Apaches still waited on the ridge even though the wagon had been moved to where Perkins had directed. Only once the troop had gone did they ride down and pillage the wagon.

★   ★   ★

'The bastards have double-crossed us,' Waters said from the corner of his mouth as he rode beside Perkins.

It was still an hour until noon, and the desert sun held a serious bite as it climbed towards its peak. The trail snaked through a narrow canyon and

139

out into a wider dry wash before it climbed a gentle slope through clumps of boulders.

Delshay and his Apaches had been shadowing them for the past hour, confirming Perkins's suspicions that the chief was about to go back on their agreement.

Perkins nodded. 'Make sure the rest of the troop is on its toes.'

Waters swung out of line and rode back along the column to see to the rest of the men. He needn't have worried, because they were all experienced and had seen all the signals that Perkins and Waters had. By the time he rode back and eased in beside his commanding officer, they all had rifles out and were prepared for what was to come.

It wasn't until they reached the boulders that the Apaches opened up on them. Even though they were expecting it, the effect of the first volley was devastating. Beside Perkins, Waters's throat seemed to erupt in a great gout of blood as a heavy caliber bullet from a Spencer tore through it, spraying blood over his commanding officer.

Angry lead hornets fizzed through the air, and Perkins flinched at the loud snap as one passed too close. Behind him, shouts of panic from his men rang out as friends and comrades died violently. Perkins saw a trooper go down with half of his face shot away, while another took two slugs to his midsection.

Wild cries from the Apaches erupted from the rocks as the gunfire rolled across the desert. Some of the troopers dived from their horses and sought cover beside the trail. Many were cut down before they'd taken two steps.

The ear-piercing screams of wounded horses added to the din. But these were professional men and all had been under fire at some stage throughout the war. Back along the column, Perkins could hear the rallying cries of Crow as he tried to get a bunch of troopers to concentrate their fire. Then his shouts stopped as he took a Spencer bullet to his chest and another through his left eye.

All around Perkins, troopers were dying. Some looked to him for direction, only to be met by silence. For the first time in his career, Perkins froze and didn't know how to save his men. And as the screams and gunfire reached a crescendo, he did the only thing that he could. He ran.

Ten minutes later it was all over. Only three men escaped the massacre laid out by Delshay. The Apache lost five warriors.

Of the three rebels who survived, one was Perkins.

★　★　★

Late in the afternoon, Savage estimated that he was perhaps two miles from the lookout rock, and decided that the best time to scout Fort Jackson to see exactly what was what would be under the cover of darkness. By chance, he was unable to wait for dark.

Two troopers on foam-flecked horses came blundering hell-for-leather out of a draw and almost rode Savage and the pinto down. They hauled back on their reins and brought their mounts to a sliding stop.

Savage rested his hand on the butt of his Remington and said, 'You fellers look like you're in a hurry.'

'Get out of our way,' one of the riders bleated. 'We gotta get back to the fort before we wind up dead too.'

Savage left the pinto where it was. 'What do you mean?'

'Like the rest of the troop that went out with Perkins,' he answered, 'they're all dead.'

'Not Perkins, though,' the other man snorted. 'That son of a bitch lit outa there like a scalded cat. I'd like to put a bullet between that bastard's eyes.'

Suddenly the other man's eyes lit up in recognition. 'Say, aren't you that feller who escaped from the fort?'

The Remington seemed to leap into

Savage's fist and it came up level, cocked and ready to fire. 'Don't you fellers get too excited,' Savage warned. 'I want you to tell me what happened.'

'Perkins thought he could make a deal with the Apaches,' the first man explained, a disgusted look on his face. 'He took rifles from the fort to help make it happen. He thought if they got the rifles, then they would be happy with that and join with us. Dumb son of a bitch. None of us liked the idea, but what could we do? He was our commanding officer. Then the Apaches double-crossed him and ambushed us. The rest you know.'

'What about Shelby? What's happened to him?'

'Perkins had him locked up and was gonna try him for treason,' the first man explained.

Savage shook his head. *Dumb son of a bitch.* He holstered the Remington. 'Come on, then. Let's go.'

'What?'

'I'm comin' with you back to the

fort,' he explained. 'Who did Perkins leave in charge?'

'Esa Brown.'

Nodding, Savage asked, 'Where do you fellers stand now? Are you still loyal to the coward that ran out on you, or are you willin' to follow Shelby?'

'We'll follow Shelby,' the second man said.

'Even if he wants to give the cause away and go home?'

They looked at each other and nodded. 'We've had just about enough of all this,' the first man told Savage. 'We wouldn't mind goin' home ourselves.'

'So then you'll help me?'

'Do what?'

'Bust Shelby out of the guardhouse?'

'We will,' they agreed.

'What are your names?'

'Fox,' said the first man. He was only young, with a babyish face and red hair.

'I'm Munn,' said the second man, who was in his thirties with dirty blond hair.

'Let's go, then.'

11

The sentry they found at lookout rock was bound and gagged so that he wouldn't make any noise. Then Munn stayed behind to take up his position while Savage and Fox closed on the fort under the cover of darkness.

The night air of the desert was cold, and the cloudless sky did little to help. The moon was a silver sliver in the sky surrounded by blinking pinpricks of light. Savage and Fox dismounted from their horses while still a good distance out and led them in on foot, their boots making soft squeaking sounds in the desert sand.

They stopped in the darkened shadow of an adobe building where they left their horses ground-hitched. There were no sentries visible, though that didn't mean that they weren't there.

'You lead the way,' Savage told Fox. 'Just remember this. If by some chance you change your mind and try to betray me, I'll put a bullet in your head before you can blink.'

'I ain't gonna cause you no trouble,' Fox told him. 'I just want this to be over. After what I saw happen today, I've had enough.'

'Get movin'.'

Savage followed Fox closely as they flitted from shadow to shadow until they reached the wall of the guardhouse. Savage leaned against it and could feel the heat of the day still seeping from the hard mud-brick wall.

They paused there briefly then Fox moved around to the front where the door was located. There were some muffled words followed by a dull thud. Fox reappeared, dragging the guard-house sentry by his arms.

'It's all clear,' he whispered harshly as he grabbed the unconscious man's campaign hat and put it on. Then he held up the keys he'd relieved the guard of. 'I'll stand watch while you talk to the general.'

Fox stood outside the door while Savage slipped into the guardhouse. He moved his way along the dimly lit corridor and came to a stop halfway along.

'General?' he said cautiously. 'General Shelby?'

'Who is it?' a quiet voice came back from behind the second door along.

'Savage.'

'What are you doing here? Is Simeon with you?'

Savage unlocked the door and opened it. Shelby stepped out into the hallway and looked about.

'Where's Simeon? I sent him after you to warn you about what Perkins was up to.'

'He's dead,' Savage told Shelby and went on to relate how he'd found the captain and also about his brush with Cochise.

'Damn it,' Shelby cursed. 'We need

to get some men together and stop Perkins from delivering those guns to the Apaches.'

'It's too late for that,' Savage informed him. 'They already have them. The only problem is that it backfired spectacularly. Delshay double-crossed him once he had the rifles. They rode into an ambush and were slaughtered.'

A rage burned in Shelby that caused him to tremble as though ready to explode. 'All those men, *my* men,' he said through gritted teeth. 'I hope the bastard died slowly.'

'Accordin'' to the two survivors I found, the yellow son of a bitch lit out when things got tough.'

That seemed to surprise Shelby, because the man he knew had shown tremendous courage under fire. He dismissed the thought and said to Savage, 'Come with me.'

'Where are we goin'?'

'To take back my damned fort.'

★ ★ ★

Esa Brown was seated behind the commanding officer's desk in the adobe building used as Shelby's headquarters. He was dreaming about the new Confederacy when the three of them burst in.

'What the hell . . . ?' he blurted out as he stared down the barrel of the six-gun in Savage's fist.

'Get up, Esa,' Shelby snarled. 'You and that damned traitorous bastard Perkins are done.'

Esa stood up, his jaw set defiantly. 'You won't get away with this. When the major gets back, he'll have you all shot.'

'He isn't coming back,' Shelby informed him. 'The damned fool got his entire command slaughtered by the Apaches.'

Esa's face paled. 'I don't believe it.'

'You better damn well believe it. I was there. I saw the yeller dog run out on us with his tail between his legs,' Fox supplied.

Esa was stunned.

'Take him away and lock him up,

trooper Fox,' Shelby ordered. 'I'll work out what to do with him in the morning.'

Fox escorted the still numb sergeant out, and Shelby turned to Savage.

'Thank you for your help, Mr. Savage,' he said gratefully. 'But I wondered if I might impose myself and request your further help?'

Savage nodded. 'You'd best tell me what you want.'

Shelby's expression grew stern and he started to pace about the room. 'With the death of Ben Simeon, I lost the main person upon whom I could place my total trust beyond any doubt. I'd like you to take his place until I can get things back in order.'

'I don't mean any offense, General, but I ain't no Johnny Reb.'

'And that's why I want your help. Because you aren't one of them.'

Savage thought for a moment. 'What do you propose to do?'

'Come tomorrow, I'll have a special parade of those who are left, after which

I'll form them up and ride to the nearest fort, where I'll officially surrender.'

'We'll need to get past the Apaches first,' Savage observed.

'I was hoping that if I give you a couple of good men, you might ride scout for the column.'

'Are you prepared to get more of your men killed? Sure as shootin' they'll be called upon to fight.'

'I'm aware of that.'

'And more than likely you'll be outnumbered.'

A wry smile crossed Shelby's face. 'Something we're more than used to.'

'All right then, I'll scout.'

'Thank you.'

The door banged back and Fox staggered in, blood streaming from a gash to his head. Savage hurried to his side to steady him.

'What happened?' he asked as he guided him to a seat.

'The son of a bitch distracted me long enough to belt me. After he did that, he ran off into the dark. He's out in the desert now somewhere.'

'Stay here,' Shelby ordered Fox, and made for the door. Savage followed close behind him.

They were halfway across the dusty parade ground when a coyote sounded out in the darkness of the desert. Savage put his hand on Shelby's arm to halt him.

Shelby felt the tension in Savage, and when he spoke it was almost a whisper. 'What's wrong?'

'Have your men stand to, General. Delshay and his Apaches have arrived.'

★ ★ ★

Munn didn't stand a chance when Delshay and his warriors came through. After the day he'd had, the last thing he should be doing was standing watch. He was drained, spent, and he fought hard to keep his eyes open. It was a battle he lost convincingly, and was soon emitting soft snores.

The darkness produced a wraith-like shadow moving silently like fluid over the rocks. The Apache's left hand clamped on Munn's chin and lifted it, exposing the flesh of his throat. The knife was drawn swiftly across it, biting deep, and brought forth a flood of warm blood that spilled down the trooper's front.

The Apache cast the lifeless form aside, then moved swiftly to kill the trussed sentry who lay writhing on the ground in an attempt to get away. After he'd finished his grisly work, he stood upon the rock and signaled the waiting horde, which swept over the ridge and into the valley beyond.

★ ★ ★

Esa had no idea of the direction he was running in, or where it would take him, as he stumbled once more. All he knew was that if he stayed, he would die in front of a firing squad. Parts of his body throbbed where the wicked spines of a prickly pear were embedded.

The faint moonlight hadn't cast sufficient illumination for him to see the clump of cactus, and he'd tripped and fallen upon it. When he'd managed to regain his feet, he'd hurriedly pulled some of the painful barbs from his hands, arms, legs, and even his face. Although the night air was cool, sweat still coursed down his face, mixing with the blood that seeped from the wounds on his cheeks.

Esa had decided to go as far as he could before daylight, then find a place to hide for the daylight hours. The last thing he wanted was to be caught out in the open, on foot, by the Yavapai.

As he blundered on, Esa was totally unaware of the three figures closing the gap to his left and right. The Apache on his left crashed into him with such force that it stunned him and took all the air from his lungs.

By the time he regained his senses, it was too late, and all three of the warriors had him imprisoned in their grasp. Worst of all, Esa was still alive.

12

It had taken the remainder of the night, but when the sun rose over Fort Jackson the following morning, all was in readiness for an attack. Shelby had tried to plug the gaps in the perimeter by whatever means necessary. Wagons and even furniture had been used.

His men were spread thin, though they were well armed and had enough ammunition for a lengthy siege. What they didn't have was enough water, the source of which was outside of their perimeter.

The desert was eerily silent as the troopers waited for it to come alive with the piercing shrieks and war cries of attacking Apaches. But the shrieks they did hear weren't those of mounted or even dismounted attackers. They were the screams of Esa Brown.

Delshay had him staked out and naked. They made sure he remained conscious as they started to slice off his eyelids, bringing forth his first screams. They followed it up by using cactus spines like miniature skewers and stuck them into his eyeballs.

The Apaches toyed with him for the next hour with knives, hot coals and whatever else they could think of to prolong the pain. Eventually his screams became a hoarse croak. They finished it off by tying him to a pony and taking him for a drag.

* * *

'It sounds like they've finished with whoever they were torturing,' Shelby observed.

A shout brought attention to the level ground at the front of the fort where the trail came in. An Apache rode hell-for-leather through the cactus, dragging something behind his mustang. It didn't take long to work out what it was as it bounced over the desert floor.

Riding a large arc, the warrior turned and swept back along the barricade at the front of the fort. Once he reached the trail, the Indian released his burden and kept riding. What remained of Esa Brown came to a halt right in the middle. So stunned were the onlookers that no one fired a shot.

Savage cursed under his breath and raised the Yellow Boy to his shoulder. He sighted along the octagonal barrel and lined it up on the retreating Apache's muscular bronze back. He squeezed the trigger and the rifle bucked, spewing blue-gray gunsmoke from its muzzle. Through the cloud in front of him, Savage saw the warrior throw up his arms and fall when the .44 Henry slug blew his spine in half.

'He won't be doing that again in a hurry,' Shelby said. 'Good shot.'

Two soldiers jumped the barricade and ran out to see whose the body was.

When they left it there, Savage had a fair idea.

'It's Brown, General,' one of the men called to Shelby.

He nodded. 'Got his comeuppance, if you ask me.'

Savage kept his eyes on the desert. In his mind, he tried to work out what Delshay might do.

'What do you think, Mr. Savage?' Shelby asked.

'Just call me Savage, General. No need for 'Mister'.'

'Fine, but what do you think?'

'Your fort is bordered on three sides by broken ground,' Savage explained. 'The fourth side, out along the trail there to the west, is pretty much level goin'. So if Delshay wants to make a mounted assault on this place, then that will be the only ground suitable for his horses.'

'My thoughts exactly,' Shelby acknowledged. 'Although I don't think that he'll throw all of his braves against us there.'

Savage shook his head. 'If I was him, I'd put my best shots on that high ground to the north where they can fire down into the fort. I'd make a light charge with mounted warriors from the west along the flat ground, and then use a heavier assault force over the broken ground to the east and south once we were engaged with the mounted charge.'

Shelby liked Savage's thinking and acknowledged it. 'I could have used you in my brigade. That's a sound strategy. Let's hope that our friend out there doesn't think like that.'

'I guess we're about to find out,' Savage said, nodding at a low ridge to the southwest.

Turning to look, Shelby saw the line of mounted warriors, maybe thirty in total.

Savage drew his gaze away and looked to the north. He studied the high ground with the practiced eye of a commanding officer. Beside him, Shelby started to issue orders to his men.

Straining to make out anything suspicious, Savage's eyes roamed back and forth until he started to feel relieved that there was nothing to worry about. He was about to turn back when he caught the flicker of movement on the slope.

'Get down!' Savage shouted as he lunged at Shelby.

Surprised, he swiveled to look at Savage but was tackled solidly to the hard earth of the parade ground. 'What the . . . ?' was all Shelby got out before the slope came alive with puffs of gunsmoke closely followed by the flat reports of the rifles. Most of the first volley missed, but there were a few troopers who were unlucky enough to stop lead. Their cries of pain drifted across the fort grounds as more shots were fired from above.

'I suggest we find ourselves some cover, Savage,' Shelby said, dragging himself to his feet.

Both men ran towards one of the barrack buildings, bullets whipping

161

through the air, cracking loudly as they passed close. They took refuge against its earthen wall and gathered themselves.

'It would seem that you're partially right,' Shelby gasped, sucking in some deep breaths.

'Let's hope I wasn't totally right,' Savage said.

A trooper who had run across the parade ground to help a wounded comrade took a bullet in his throat, which left a gaping exit wound. He stopped in his tracks and blood fountained from a severed artery. Slowly he sank to the ground and lay still.

'Bastards,' Shelby snarled.

The volley of fire from the high ground acted as a signal for the mounted Apaches to start their attack, and they came off the ridge screaming and whooping. Sporadic rifle fire came from the front barricade but was quickly quelled with a snapped command from the sergeant in charge.

'Can I make a suggestion, General?' Savage asked.

'By all means, but make it quick,' Shelby told him.

'Do you have any sharpshooters under your command?'

'A couple.'

'It might pay to put them on one of the roofs takin' shots at the shooters on the high ground,' Savage suggested. 'Might even get a few of them. At worst it'll keep their heads down.'

Shelby nodded. 'A sound idea. I'll see to it.'

Savage watched as he disappeared.

A volley of gunfire erupted at the front barricade, and the charging line of Apaches was met with a hail of lead. Horses and riders fell as it scythed through their ranks. The almost human screams of the wounded animals brought visions of scarred battlefields from the war.

A second volley brought down more and stopped the probe in its tracks. It was then that gunfire erupted on the east side. It appeared that Delshay had read Savage's mind. He levered a round into the Winchester's breech and ran to join the troopers as they tried to defend against the swarming Apaches.

*　★　★

Belly down amongst the rocks, perhaps half a mile from Fort Jackson, lay Major Christopher Perkins. He watched in silence as the wave of riders hit the front of the fort. He saw men die on both sides of the fight. He saw the puffs of gunsmoke from the high ground and he saw something else that the defenders couldn't. He could see the hidden warriors scattered throughout the broken ground of gullies, rocks, and cactus to the east and estimated their numbers to be around one hundred.

Since the meeting with the guns, Delshay's numbers had swelled some; and Perkins figured that even though the soldiers were well trained, the

Apaches would eventually overwhelm them. As he watched, the charge of the mounted warriors came to an abrupt halt from the fire they came under.

However, their job was done. The distraction seemed to have worked, and as that attack faltered, the Indians hidden in the broken ground rose up and commenced their attack. He stayed until the front wave breached the perimeter, then he slid backward out of sight to where his horse was. He stood up, climbed into the saddle, and rode away with the *pop-pop* of gunfire still sounding in the distance.

13

Savage wiped at the thin rivulet of blood that ran down the right side of his face with his sleeve. The cut in his left shoulder burned and the one on his back felt much the same. On both sides of him were dead troopers. One had an arrow through his throat and the other had taken a bullet to his chest.

He rested the Winchester on the barricade and reloaded it, then did the same with his Remington. The fort had been hit hard, but for the moment the gunfire had ceased. All around him there were dead soldiers and Indians. Once the Apaches had breached the perimeter, the fighting became ugly.

Vicious hand-to-hand fighting had broken out at that point, with troopers using anything they could to try and stop the overwhelming force. Savage remembered one incident where a desperate young trooper had bitten into the neck of his attacker, bringing forth a spray of blood.

Somehow they'd held, and the Apaches had withdrawn to melt back into the desert landscape. However, from the amount of dust he'd seen being raised, Savage guessed there were a lot more out there.

'I see you're still with us?' Shelby said as he walked up behind Savage.

Savage looked up at him and nodded. 'It was a close-run thing, though.'

'All around I'm afraid,' Shelby agreed. 'Although this side seems to have taken the worst of it.' He shook his head when he looked around and took in his dead men lying about the fort.

Savage noticed the blood on his sleeve. 'Are you OK?'

'What, this?' he said, indicating the wound on his left arm. 'Just a scratch. You seem to have a few yourself.'

'I was wounded worse in the Shenandoah Valley,' Savage said honestly. Then he asked, 'How many did you lose?'

'Between dead and wounded, fifty men. Fifty!' The pain was evident on his face. 'If they hit us like that again, I'm not sure if the fort can hold.'

Savage looked about. Smoke hung heavily in the air, as almost everything timber had burned from the fire arrows that Delshay's warriors had used. He saw troopers helping the wounded and others removing the dead to the center of the parade ground. There were two piles for soldiers and Apaches, with the former being the larger one.

'Hey, General, lookee there,' a trooper called out to Shelby.

Both he and Savage looked to where the man was pointing and saw that an Apache with a white cloth tied to a stick had appeared on the trail.

'Care to take a walk?' Shelby asked.

Savage nodded. 'Why not.'

They climbed the front perimeter and walked a short distance along the trail before stopping. The Apache came closer and stopped in front of them both.

'I am Delshay, Chief of the Yavapai-Apache,' he said in an arrogant tone. 'Are you the white chief?'

'I am,' said Shelby.

'Good. You will give us guns and we will go. Let you live.'

Shelby smiled coldly. 'You can go to hell.'

'Then you all die.'

'If you ain't noticed,' Savage challenged, 'you lost a lot of men when you attacked. What makes you think you'll be able to kill us all?'

The Apache held up his left hand as a sign, and suddenly the ridges and uneven ground surrounding Fort Jackson sprouted Apaches. 'After first fight, more join with Delshay,' he snapped. 'You give guns and you live.'

Savage stared hard at the Indian and shifted his stance. He frowned and glanced around. He could feel that something wasn't right, and at that moment he saw a flicker of movement in the rocks not far from the trail. It was a trap.

'How fast can you run, General?'
'What?'

Savaged brought up the Yellow Boy so that the muzzle was no more than six inches from the startled Indian's face and fired. The Apache's head snapped back as the rifle slug smashed through his nose and out the back of his head with such violence that it seemed to explode.

Savage worked the lever on the rifle and swung about to face the rocks where he'd seen the movement. With a shout of rage, an Indian leaped from behind the rock he'd been sheltered by and aimed one of the Spencers that had been taken from the wagon at him.

Firing from the hip, Savage's next shot hit the Indian in his midsection, doubling him over. He didn't fire a second shot. He was too busy running for cover.

'What the hell did you do that for?' Shelby gasped when they ducked down in behind the barricade, bullets snapping overhead.

'Because it was a trap and the son of a bitch wasn't Delshay,' Savage explained.

'Are you sure?'

'About as sure as I can be.'

Once more, the Apaches swarmed the defenses and the defenders drove them back after more vicious fighting. Heavy casualties were taken by both sides, but still the Apaches held the upper hand.

Due to good fortune rather than luck, Savage remained alive and for the most part wound-free. He sat on an ammunition crate while all about him lay the dead and wounded. Against all odds, the defenders had held again.

A tired-looking trooper with blood stains on his uniform approached Savage. 'The general wants to see you.'

Savage frowned. 'Is he OK?'

'He's wounded,' was all he said.

He found Shelby inside an intact building, lying on a table while a trooper worked at removing an arrow from his shoulder.

'There . . . there you are.' He winced as the trooper probed around the arrow with a knife. 'Take over command for a while, will you?'

Savage shook his head. 'It needs to be one of your men. They ain't gonna like a Yank givin' them orders.'

'Damn it, man,' Shelby hissed, his face twisted with anger and pain, 'just do it. You were a captain for chrissakes. What these men need at the moment is a leader until I'm back on my feet.'

'All right. But only until then.'

'It's ready to come out now, General,' the trooper warned his commanding officer.

'Just wait,' he snapped. 'Savage, you'll need to bring in the perimeter because we're spread too thin.'

'Already thought about that,' he admitted to Shelby. 'Don't worry, I'll take care of it.'

'Make sure the men are ready.'

'It'll be fine. They won't be back

today. They'll regroup and hit us again at first light.'

'Maybe we can hold them again,' Shelby said, trying to sound convincing.

'Maybe.'

Savage left then. There were so many things to do to prepare for what was to come, all the while knowing that the next attack would be the last.

* * *

It was almost dark when Savage was approached by a grizzled sergeant and a tall, thin corporal. 'Can we have a word with you for a moment, Savage?' the sergeant asked in a deep voice.

'Sure . . . ?'

'Mahoney,' he said. 'This is Phelps.'

Savage nodded. 'What's on your mind?'

'We . . . the men have been talkin' amongst ourselves, and we've come to the conclusion that there ain't no way that any of us are gonna get outa this alive.'

Shrugging his shoulders, Savage said, 'You never know. We might be able to hold them out.'

'You and me been soldiers long enough to know horse shit when it's spoke, Savage,' Mahoney stated. 'We have a grand total of thirty fit men left. That second attack chewed up a lot of good men. There ain't no way in hell we're gettin' outa this.'

Mahoney was right and Savage knew it.

'However, two men just might be able to get through the Apaches,' the sergeant continued.

'Spell it out, Mahoney,' Savage commanded.

'We talked it over, and we think that you should take the general and get out.'

'Now why would you want that?' Savage asked, his face passive.

'We believe that if anyone deserves to get outa here, it's the general,' Mahoney said. 'We've been fightin' for him for years now and we figure that if this is the last time, then we should have somethin' to show for it at the end instead of corpses.'

'Why don't you try to get him out?'

Mahoney shook his head. 'Nope, it has to be you. You ain't one of us.'

'How do you propose we do it?' Savage asked him.

'You leave that up to us,' he remarked. 'Along the southern perimeter of the fort, there's a dry wash. It's close enough so we know there won't be any Apaches hidin' in it. It should be deep enough too. You'll need to be at the perimeter in an hour or so with horses. You'll slip out and into the wash and wait until the diversion that we'll mount is underway.'

'What diversion?'

'You'll know it,' Mahoney assured him. 'So will you do it?'

'All right, I'll do it.'

★ ★ ★

Savage readied the horses first, then took them to where he'd last seen

Shelby. Inside, he found the general sitting up, shirt open revealing the bloodied bandage, and arguing with Mahoney.

'Blast your eyes, Mahoney,' Shelby hissed at the sergeant. 'I'm still in command here, and if I say I'm staying, then I'm staying.'

Mahoney ignored him and looked across at Savage. 'Are the horses ready?'

'Yeah.'

He fixed his angry gaze on Savage and snapped harshly, 'I can't believe you agreed to this.'

'The way I see it is that we're all most likely gonna die anyway,' Savage explained, 'and I'd rather die out there doin' somethin' worthwhile. And Mahoney there convinced me that you were worthwhile. Who knows, we may even make it.'

Shelby set his jaw firm and said belligerently, 'My place is here with my men.'

'Let's get one thing straight, you stubborn son of a bitch,' Savage hissed.

'You're comin'. Even if I have to bend a damn gun barrel over that hard head of yours and carry you. Your men realize they're gonna die here. Let them do it fightin' for somethin'. Now when you're ready, I'll be outside with the horses.'

A couple of minutes later, Shelby walked out of the small building. Nothing was said as he and Savage walked the horses over to the south side. Before they exited, Shelby turned to his sergeant and said, 'God be with you, Mahoney.'

As they shook hands, Savage heard him say, 'I think God has already left here, sir.'

Mahoney looked at Savage. 'Get him through, Yank.'

Savage nodded. 'Give 'em hell, Johnny Reb.'

Then, without looking back, they led their animals out into the darkness.

14

Ten men sat atop their horses and waited. Every one of them had volunteered for this final suicidal duty. Ten were all that Mahoney had wanted. It should be a sufficient number to carry out their task. His hope was to create enough chaos and draw the Apaches in to provide a small opening in the ring for Savage and Shelby to slip through.

The horses stomped and snorted as they sensed something in the air.

'Phelps, don't forget to blow the ammunition store. We don't want the enemy gettin' their hands on more rifles and ammunition now, do we?'

'Consider it done,' Phelps assured him.

Mahoney called out to a man who carried a bugle. 'Wake the bastards up, Junior,' he ordered.

The young man put the bugle to his lips and blew the charge. Mahoney had instructed the volunteers to wait until he gave the signal. He let Junior go on for a little longer before he raised his hand and shouted, 'Charge!'

The ten volunteers, with Mahoney at their head, rode out into the darkness and to their deaths.

*   *   *

Shelby went to move forward, but a hand from Savage stopped him.

'Wait,' he whispered harshly.

The sound of the bugle rang loud in the crisp night desert air. Around them, objects moved as the hidden Apaches came alive. Sudden gunfire started to fill the night with cries of alarm. Somewhere a loud rebel yell pierced the darkness, and another flurry of shots rang out.

From the blackness loomed a shadow, and Savage's hand flashed to the Remington on his hip. It came out of the holster and he squeezed the trigger. The orange tongue of flame that spewed forth lit the immediate area, and Savage could see the Apache's face. The Indian staggered from the slug's impact and fell forward.

'Shelby, get on your horse!' Savage shouted. 'Now!'

Both men mounted and spurred their horses wickedly. They lunged forward and were soon running hard through the desert away from the flashes and pops of the receding gunfire.

A figure lunged at Shelby from behind a saguaro, but the general was on to it and fired his six-gun point-blank into the attacking Indian. Then another appeared and grabbed at Savage, hooking onto his leg and almost dislodging him from the saddle. He lashed out with the Remington and caught the Indian across the head as he was being dragged along by the fast-moving paint. The Apache cried out and fell away.

More figures moved in the dark, and Savage emptied his Remington at them.

Ahead, Shelby did the same, his gun-flashes illuminating the dark.

Then the desert stopped moving and the sound of gunfire disappeared. They were clear.

*   *   *

Delshay was far from happy. All about him were dead warriors — *his* warriors; and it gnawed at him like a festering wound. He looked at the blackened hole in the ground where the ammunition store had been blown up. Taking on the white-eyes' fort had cost him too many men. By rights, he should have stopped the attack before it ever got this far, but the Apache chief's stubborn pride hadn't let him and this was the result. He looked up at the clear blue early-morning sky and saw the vultures already starting to circle.

A shirtless warrior jogged up to him, the muscles on his torso rippling as he moved across the corpse-strewn parade ground. 'Two of the white-eyes have escaped,' he said, coming to a stop before the Apache chief.

Delshay's face screwed up with bitterness. 'How?'

'I do not know. In the dark. They killed some warriors as they rode clear.'

The Apache chief looked once more at the dead scattered all around. Such a waste of his brave warriors. Then he looked at the dead white men, and all of a sudden the whole thing sickened him.

'Let them go,' Delshay murmured, all of his fight now gone.

'But . . . '

'I said let them go,' he commanded. 'Enough blood has been spilled in revenge. Maybe too much.'

The warrior nodded and walked away, leaving Delshay alone among the dead.

* * *

By the end of the day, Shelby swayed in his saddle like a drunk riding home after a day in the saloon. He had a raging fever that indicated that his wound was becoming infected. His face glistened with sweat and his words were starting to slur.

Savage knew that they needed to find somewhere to lay up so he could see to him, or there was a good chance that Shelby would die. He found a place not long before dusk along a shallow springfed creek. Ten yards back from the water was a steep cut with an overhang where they could make camp.

Once he had the horses tethered and a small fire going, Savage crossed to where Shelby lay. 'How are you feelin'?'

Shelby shivered uncontrollably as fever ravaged his body. 'Great.'

'I'd better have a look at that wound of yours,' Savage said, leaning forward.

'How long do you plan on staying here?'

Savage opened his shirt, and as he did so said, 'I didn't see no dust or anythin', so I'd say we're safe here for the time bein'.'

Shelby stiffened as his wound was probed and prodded.

'I'm gonna have to open that back up to release some of the infection,' Savage informed the general. 'It'll hurt like a bitch but it needs to be done.'

'Can't make me feel any worse.'

Savage took his knife and placed it in the fire to sterilize the blade, then went to the stream to collect some fresh water in a canteen and washed the soiled bandages. When he returned, he put the blade aside to cool.

'Are you ready?'

Shelby nodded apprehensively.

Taking up the knife, Savage clenched his jaw and said hoarsely, 'Keep still.'

He leaned as much weight as possible upon Shelby to hold him steady, then pushed the knife blade into the festering mess and released the stinking build-up of pus. Beneath him, Shelby writhed and cried out from the acute burning pain that seared into his brain.

Ten minutes later, with the wound cleaned as best he could, Savage placed the knife blade back into the fire. He left it there until the blade glowed red, then placed it against the exposed wound. The general's deafening roar was cut short as it all became too much and he passed out.

*　*　*

Morgan, Stark and Willis were outlaws. Not famous ones by any stretch, but outlaws nonetheless, and were wanted for stagecoach hold-ups, bank jobs, and numerous killings. At this point in time, they were headed for a small settlement called Phoenix.

It had just turned dark when the rider came upon them camped out in a draw by a shallow stream. Their first indication of his presence was the sound of horseshoe striking rock.

'Hello the camp, I'm coming in,' the rider called out, his voice unmistakably Southern.

All three men stood up and kept their hands where they could reach their six-guns in case of trouble.

'Come on in,' Morgan called back. 'Just keep your hands away from your hardware or we'll shoot you down.'

When the rider rode in close enough, he dismounted and walked into the firelight, where the three outlaws could see him.

'Well lookee what we got here,' Morgan guffawed. 'It Robert E. Lee hisself. All duded up in his Reb uniform.'

Perkins stood motionless and studied the three men.

'Damn, Morg,' Willis joined in, 'if you ain't right at that. 'What's your name, Reb?'

'Perkins.'

'Haven't you heard? The war's over,' Morgan remarked.

'You don't say.'

'What you all doin' way out here anyways?' Stark asked.

'Riding,' Perkins said. 'Where are you men headed?'

'Phoenix,' Morgan answered.

'Never heard of it.'

'It's a new settlement. Ain't even got any law yet,' Willis informed him.

Perkins looked at the coffee pot on the boil. 'Coffee smells good,' he commented.

'You want some?' Morgan asked.

'Sure.'

'Take a seat and Stark will get you some.'

The four men were seated around the fire when Perkins asked, 'Are you men outlaws?'

At first, they were surprised by the question, not expecting a stranger to ask such a thing considering there were three of them.

Morgan's gaze grew hard and he said, 'Yeah, we're outlaws.'

'I thought so,' Perkins said nonchalantly.

'What's it to you?' Morgan asked.

Perkins shrugged. 'No reason. Who's in charge?'

'What?' asked Stark.

'I said who's in charge?'

'I am,' Morgan snapped.

Without warning, Perkins drew his six-gun and shot Morgan in the face. The outlaw's head snapped back and his arms flew into the air, releasing the mug he'd held, and it dropped to the ground at the edge of the darkness.

Perkins shifted his aim to Willis. 'Who's in charge?'

The outlaw's mouth opened and closed. 'Ahh . . . ahh . . . '

Perkins thumbed the hammer back on his gun. The ratchet sound was loud in the tense silence. 'Who?'

'You,' Stark blurted out. 'You're in charge.'

With a cold smile on his face, Perkins said, 'That's right. I'm in charge, and you men best keep that in mind.'

He switched his gaze to the body of Morgan and guessed that the dead outlaw would be around the same size as him. He signaled to the other two and ordered them, 'Get the clothes off your friend there and bring them to me. I won't be needing this uniform now.'

15

It was two days before Shelby was ready to ride. After Savage had released the poison, it had taken until late the following day for the fever to break. Then he'd needed rest to further recover from his wound.

They were sitting by the fire on the last evening making plans to ride out the next day, eating part of an antelope that Savage had shot. They'd needed food, Shelby more so, and Savage deemed the risk worth the gunshot.

As they were eating, Shelby said, 'There's been something that's intrigued me ever since we met, Savage.'

'What's that?'

'You fought for the Union, but you speak like a Texan.'

'That's 'cause I come from Texas,'

Savage told him. 'I may be Texan, but I believed that I was doin' the right thing when I joined.'

'Did you lose everything while you were gone?' Shelby inquired. 'Like the rest when the carpetbaggers moved in?' There was a trace of harshness to his voice.

Savage thought for a moment before answering. 'You could say that.'

'What happened? Did you get back to Texas and find out you'd been fighting for the wrong side?' He thought of Amy.

'Shenandoah Valley back in '64,' Savage started. 'My commanding officer sent me out to find Carver's Raiders, who were in the area.'

Shelby nodded. 'He was an out-and-out killer.'

'Yeah,' Savage agreed. 'We found him outside a town called Bender's Hollow. He'd just finished razing it. Carver and some others got away and I was almost killed by him.'

Shelby listened in silence.

'Just before I got home to Summerton last year, him and his gang hit the bank there. People were killed, and they took a woman when they escaped. It was my wife. It was me who found her.'

'I'm sorry,' Shelby said softly.

'So were they,' Savage replied.

A heavy silence hung over the camp before Savage broke it. 'Do you reckon you'll be right to ride tomorrow?'

'I think so. This food will help regain some of my strength. Where are we headed?'

'Fort Craig,' Savage answered. 'Before all of this started, I was originally commissioned to find that damned half-breed killer, Rios. So I guess that's the best place.'

'OK.'

'You'll be able to get a decent sawbones to look at that wound of yours too.'

'Fine. Tomorrow it is.'

★   ★   ★

They broke camp and rode out shortly after first light. The desert was cool at that time of day and the air crisp and clean. There were no clouds in the pale blue sky, and the sun would soon bring a scorching heat to the rest of the day.

They maintained a steady pace, and had traveled for four hours when Savage called a stop. The horses were rested in the lee of a steep embankment while Savage climbed high enough to check their back trail. It seemed clear and he stumbled back down, kicking up a small cloud of dust as he went.

'Our back trail looks clear,' he informed Shelby.

'Maybe the Apache ain't bothering to follow us.'

'Let's hope so.'

They stayed and rested in the shade for a while longer before leaving. As the day wore on, it became hotter, and even the slight breeze felt hot on exposed skin. Then trouble appeared to raise its ugly head.

Shelby sighted the black specks first,

circling high above the desert. 'Hey, Savage, what do you make of that?' he asked, pointing at the circling birds.

They drew their mounts to a stop while Savage studied the vultures. 'Whatever it is, it can't be good.'

Savage unsheathed the Yellow Boy and levered a round into the breech, then eased the pinto forward once more.

What they found was the partially naked body of a man. The buzzards, already well into their work, had torn strips of exposed flesh from his bloated, mottled body. At their approach, a couple of the black feathered birds had waddled off a short distance, unwilling to cede their meal.

'I wonder who you were, you poor bastard,' Savage said aloud.

He walked around the immediate vicinity and studied the ground.

'There were others here,' he pointed out to Shelby. 'You can see their marks.'

'How many?' Shelby asked as he tried

to make sense of the mess on the ground.

'I don't know,' Savage said, shrugging his shoulders. 'No more than four, maybe three.'

'A falling-out, maybe. Why else would they take his clothes?'

Savage frowned. He hadn't thought much of it until now. He walked in a large circle around the outside of the camp area but found nothing. Then he looked at the burnt-out fire and something caught his eye. He leaned down and picked up a piece of fabric with a button sewn on it and rubbed it on his shirt to clean it.

'What have you found?' Shelby asked.

Savage studied it, then passed it across to him. The general looked at it closely, then fixed them firmly on the drifter.

'It's a button off a Confederate uniform,' Shelby declared.

Savage nodded. 'No prizes for guessing whose.'

'Perkins's.'

'Yeah, Perkins's. I'd say he killed that feller for his clothes. What happened after that is anyone's guess.'

'I'd like to get my hands on that bastard,' Shelby snapped. 'I'd put a bullet in his brain without blinking an eye.'

'You ain't the only one,' Savage allowed. 'Let's keep movin'.'

That night they made a secluded camp among some brush well off the trail. Early the next morning they were up and in the saddle and headed towards Fort Craig.

★ ★ ★

'Hold up,' Savage warned Shelby as he drew the pinto to a stop.

Shelby stopped his mount beside him on the crest of a low ridge. From there they could clearly see the dust haze out on the flat.

'Indians, do you think?' asked Shelby.
'Hope not.'

As the dust cloud drew nearer, they could begin to make out the figures at the base of it. Although not clearly seen, Savage had a fair idea who they were.

'Soldiers,' he said finally. 'Come on.'

16

'Damn, Savage, what on earth have you got there?' Lieutenant Joel Porter gasped as he took in the Confederate officer.

The three men dismounted and walked a short distance away from the thirty man column to talk. 'Have you gone and captured the whole Reb army?'

'Porter, this is Major General Joseph Shelby of the — '

'Who?'

'Major General Joseph Shelby, formerly of the Confederate States of America,' Shelby stated.

'Is this guy for real?' Porter asked Savage.

'I'm afraid so, Lieutenant,' Savage confirmed. 'And it might pay to show the man a little respect.'

'But he's a Reb . . . '

'He's a man who deserves your respect, Lieutenant,' he snapped.

Porter gave Savage the look a scolded child might give his mother. 'What is it that Mr. Shelby is doin' with you?'

The two men looked at each other, and Savage looked back at Porter and sighed.

'Where do we start?'

By the time he'd finished, Porter was shaking his head at the almost unbelievable tale that he'd been told. 'Wait until the colonel hears about this.'

'Are you headed back to the fort soon?' Savage asked.

'We're on the left hook of our patrol and then we head back to Fort Craig,' Porter explained. 'We should arrive back sometime tomorrow. You can ride along if you wish to.'

'Have you got any decent coffee?' Shelby asked.

'Sure.'

'Then we ride with you.'

'I agree,' Savage seconded the decision.

* ★ ★ ★

The patrol arrived back at Fort Craig
the following afternoon. Both Savage
and Shelby were immediately taken
before Colonel Maxwell Travis, where
they once more told the extraordinary
tale. Travis frowned then turned his
gaze on Shelby.

'I'm sorry about your men, General,'
he said with sincerity.

'Thank you, Colonel.'

'Now, Mr. Savage, about Cochise?'

'He's gone, Travis,' Savage explained.
'Back to his old stompin' grounds. He
won't cause you any further problems.'

'Nevertheless, I'll have to report it,'
Travis said adamantly.

'I guess it don't mean a damn about
what that scalp hunter did?' Savage
pointed out.

'Not after the waystation,' Travis
snapped. 'As for the Yavapai . . . Well, at
least Rios won't be causing any more
problems.'

Savage knew that nothing more

would be done to the Indians. After all, they'd only killed some Rebs. But in saying that, he didn't think that they should be held totally responsible for the events that had occurred either.

'Back to you, General Shelby. What is it that you propose to do? I have absolutely no idea what to do with you,' Travis pondered the problem he faced.

'I just want to go home to Missouri, Colonel,' Shelby told him. 'I just want to go home.'

Travis stared at Shelby, deep in thought. Really, there wasn't anything to think about. He still had no idea how to handle the situation.

'Then go home you will,' he said before asking Savage. 'What about you?'

'I ain't got nothin' to go home to, Travis. You know that. However, there is somethin' I would like to take care of before I leave the territory.'

'And that is?'

'Perkins,' he replied. 'Where would

him and those two fellers go around here?'

'You might try Phoenix,' Travis answered. 'It's a new settlement, and with no law there yet, it would have to be a strong possibility. But then again, they could have headed anywhere.'

'You don't have to do it, Savage,' Shelby said. 'Your job is done. You got me here safely. Now let it go.'

Savage shook his head. 'Can't. That bastard is responsible for a lot of men dyin'. I keep seein' Mahoney and Simeon. Mahoney knew he was gonna die, and yet all he . . . they could think about was you. Nope, they deserve some retribution, and I aim to give it to them.'

'I hope it's not you on the receiving end, Savage,' Shelby said grimly.

'I don't plan to be.'

*   *   *

Three days later, after resting up and saying goodbye to Shelby, Savage rode the pinto into the new settlement of Phoenix not long before noon. It wasn't much more than a few buildings and one street; only a shadow of what it would become. It was formed by Jack Swilling, who'd fought on the side of the Confederacy in the Civil War. He'd been traveling through the Salt River Valley and recognized its potential for farming.

Savage let the pinto keep its own pace as it walked steadily along the dry street, kicking up dust. Being a new settlement, the presence of a stranger drew immediate attention, one dressed in Union blue pants and shirt even more so.

He felt curious eyes watch his progress as he continued along the street. When he saw the three horses tied to a makeshift hitch rail outside what passed for a saloon, he drew rein. It was no more than a large canvas tent with a hand-painted sign leaning against its front. Savage knew that he would find Perkins here.

He eased the pinto over to the rail and dismounted. He tied the leather reins to the cross-member and adjusted the Remington in its holster. From inside he heard the high-pitched laugh of a woman filter out through the open flap.

As Savage approached it, a drunk staggered out. Under his left arm was a black-haired woman wearing nothing more than a red corset and bloomers, her large pale breasts billowing out over the top. In his right hand, he held a half-empty bottle of watered-down whiskey.

He shouldered into Savage, and the action caused the bottle to drop to the ground and spill the rest of its contents into the dirt. He screwed up his unshaven scarred face and took his arm from around the woman.

'Stranger, you're gonna pay for that,' he snarled and brought up his fists.

With the speed of a striking rattler, Savage drew the Remington and brought it crashing down on the drunk's forehead. With a resounding crack, it split skin and produced a stream of blood that ran down the man's face. His eyes crossed and he dropped like a pole-axed steer.

The whore screamed out a protest, but Savage ignored it and pushed in through the tent flap. The bar was a rough construction of a couple of boxes with planks run across the top. The light was fair, and there were a few battered tables with customers seated at them in the confined space.

Three men sat at one of the tables to his left, one with a whore in green draped over him. All eyes had fixed onto the entrance when the whore outside had screamed, and now they were looking at Savage.

Savage strode across to the table, his Remington level and cocked. They remained unmoved at his approach. Out of the corner of his right eye, he saw the barkeep move.

'If you want to keep livin', barkeep, I'd keep away from that messenger gun,' Savage warned without looking in his direction. 'If you don't, you'll be buried with whoever else comes between me and what I aim to do.'

Perkins's face paled as he saw Savage coming toward him. He eased his hand below the table and said to Willis, 'Get rid of the whore.'

'What?'

'Do it,' he snapped.

The whore, however, didn't need to be told. One look at the purpose on Savage's face was enough to cause her to get quickly to her feet and back away.

'I see you're still alive,' Perkins sneered.

'So is Shelby,' Savage told him. 'Get your hands on the table where I can see them.'

Steadily, Perkins brought both hands up, empty.

There was movement to Savage's right and he swiveled and put a bullet into the barkeep's chest. The man staggered back against the canvas, then slumped to the dirt floor.

'He was warned,' drawled Savage. 'If you all don't want the same, I suggest you stay outa this.' His eyes focused back on the table. 'My fight is with Perkins, not with you other two. Move away.'

'What if we don't want to?' Willis snarled. 'What if . . . ?'

The Remington roared once more and a third eye appeared in Willis's forehead. The pink spray of gore from where the bullet exited stained the canvas wall behind him.

Perkins flinched at the sudden roar of the six-gun. The remaining outlaw, Stark, threw up his hands and cried, 'Wait! I'm goin'. Don't shoot, I'm goin'.'

'I see you've started without me,' a familiar voice observed from behind Savage. 'Do you mind if I join the party?'

'Suit yourself,' Savage said, shrugging his shoulders.

Shelby stepped forward with a cocked six-gun in his fist.

'You, get outa here,' Savage ordered Stark.

The frightened outlaw knocked over his chair in his haste to stand and moved quickly away.

'So what now?' Perkins asked. 'You're just going to shoot me down? Like a dog?'

'I'm not,' answered Savage. Then he motioned to Shelby. 'He is.'

He holstered the Remington and turned to leave. 'All yours, General.'

As Savage stepped outside the tent, the drunk on the ground was starting to stir. He sat up and shook his head, clearing the cobwebs.

Suddenly Shelby's six-gun roared from inside. Not once, but six times.

The drunk looked warily up at Savage, his face streaked with blood. 'What the hell was that?' he croaked.

'The end of the war,' Savage remarked.

He walked over to the pinto and waited. Shelby emerged a couple of moments later just as a small crowd started to gather. Both men remained silent as they climbed on their horses and rode out of Phoenix. About a mile or so from the settlement, the trail forked and they drew their mounts to a halt.

'I guess this is where we part company, Savage,' observed Shelby.

'Yeah, I guess,' he agreed. 'You headed back to Missouri?'

'Yes. My wife will be waiting for me.' Then he added, 'I hope. What about you? Where are you headed?'

Savage rubbed the back of his neck thoughtfully. 'I was gonna head out to California, have a look around, but . . . '

'And now?'

'I might head on back to New Mexico and see if I can pick up a trail drive and take a look up north.'

Shelby moved his horse in beside the pinto and stuck out his hand. 'Thank you. For everything. If you're ever around Missouri, come and look me up.'

'Will do,' Savage told him as he took

Shelby's hand. 'Take care, General.'

'You too, Savage. You too.'

He watched Shelby ride off, then turned the pinto east. As he rode along the dry dusty trail, Savage began to whistle 'When Johnny Comes Marching Home'.

We do hope that you have enjoyed reading this large print book.

Did you know that all of our titles are available for purchase?

We publish a wide range of high quality large print books including:
Romances, Mysteries, Classics
General Fiction
Non Fiction and Westerns

Special interest titles available in large print are:
The Little Oxford Dictionary
Music Book, Song Book
Hymn Book, Service Book

Also available from us courtesy of Oxford University Press:
Young Readers' Dictionary
(large print edition)
Young Readers' Thesaurus
(large print edition)

For further information or a free brochure, please contact us at:
Ulverscroft Large Print Books Ltd.,
The Green, Bradgate Road, Anstey,
Leicester, LE7 7FU, England.
Tel: (00 44) **0116 236 4325**
Fax: (00 44) **0116 234 0205**

THE VALERON CODE

Terrell L. Bowers

When Rodney Mason is hired by a banker to help his sister, it seems like just another job. But he finds more than he bargained for in Deliverance, Colorado. The opposition is ruthless, and the victim someone who can change his world. When an ambush leaves Rod vulnerable and unable to fight back, word is sent to his brothers and cousins. Within hours, Wyatt and Jared Valeron are dispatched to aid their kin. The odds against them mount, but a Valeron doesn't know how to quit . . .

THE BLOODY TRAIL TO REDEMPTION

Paxton Johns

English aristocrat Born Gallant is riding to Dodge City when he is attacked and left to die. Initially relieved when rescued by a lawman and his posse, they then accuse him of murder. A witness has sworn that he saw Gallant stab a Kansas senator, and it seems certain he will hang for a crime he did not commit. With the help of some old friends, Gallant uncovers a web of political intrigue and vengeance — but will he be able to unmask the true murderer?

RIMROCK RENEGADE

Ned Oaks

Released after spending five years in prison for a crime he didn't commit, Hank Chesham only wants to return home to his ranch, the Rimrock, and resume his old life. But then he discovers that he has been betrayed by both his wife, Phoebe, and his best friend, Ted Flynn, who have conspired to steal the Rimrock from him. Now Chesham has but one thing on his mind: vengeance. But before he can take action, Flynn unleashes his hired killers . . .

THE LAST GUN

Peter Wilson

Jack Crawford, badly wounded in the final action of the Civil War, returns home to discover that his parents have been massacred, and the family ranch has fallen into the hands of empire-building newcomer Vic Bannon. When Crawford becomes town sheriff, he finds himself in opposition to the ruthless Bannon, with his own brother Clay helping to force the homesteaders and farmers out of the valley. As the threat of range war looms, Crawford must defend the home he now barely recognizes, before it disappears forever.